"You're safe here. You can trust me. I'll take care of you."

Natasha stepped backward, but Dylan didn't let her step away from him. "I wish you wouldn't say that," she said. "I'm supposed to be the protector. I'm supposed to be taking care of you and your son."

"You are."

"No, I'm not. Look at me. I'm a mess. I'm standing here wishing I could just—"

"Wishing what?" He was so close she could feel his breath. "Tell me what frightens you."

Her pulse strummed in her temple, her throat, all the way through her. "This," she murmured. "You."

MALLORY KANE

A FATHER'S SACRIFICE

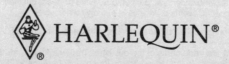

HARLEQUIN®

TORONTO • NEW YORK • LONDON
AMSTERDAM • PARIS • SYDNEY • HAMBURG
STOCKHOLM • ATHENS • TOKYO • MILAN • MADRID
PRAGUE • WARSAW • BUDAPEST • AUCKLAND

This book is for Galen.
I couldn't have done it without you.

ISBN-13: 978-0-373-88795-8
ISBN-10:   0-373-88795-7

A FATHER'S SACRIFICE

Copyright © 2007 by Rickey R. Mallory

Printed in U.S.A.

ABOUT THE AUTHOR

Mallory Kane has always loved reading and writing stories. She credits her love of books to her mother, a librarian, who taught her that books are a precious resource and should be treated with loving respect. Her father and grandfather were steeped in the Southern tradition of oral history, and could hold an audience spellbound for hours with their storytelling skills. She aspires to be as good a storyteller as her father. When she's not writing, Mallory creates and designs greeting cards. She lives in Mississippi with her husband, Michael, and their two cats.

For more information about Mallory and all her book projects, visit her Web site at www.mallorykane.com. Mallory loves to hear from readers. Write her at rickey_m@bellsouth.net.

Books by Mallory Kane

HARLEQUIN INTRIGUE

*Ultimate Agents

CAST OF CHARACTERS

Dylan Stryker—The brilliant neurosurgeon will sacrifice anything, even his own life, to give his toddler son the ability to walk.

Natasha Rudolph—The beautiful FBI agent has only one weakness—close spaces. When she's forced to face her worst fear to protect Dylan Stryker and his son, an old enemy targets her for revenge.

Ben Stryker—Dylan's three-year-old son is a pint-sized image of his handsome father. He can't walk without the computer-driven braces invented by his father.

Tom Johnson—One of the best hackers in the world, Tom isn't satisfied with mere wealth. He wants power. Stealing Dylan Stryker's super-soldier technology will give him both.

Alfred Mintz—Stryker's ex-POW security chief has made his home into an impenetrable fortress. Anyone wanting to harm Dylan or Ben will have to go through him.

Jerry Campbell—The talented bioengineer and computer expert is the best at what he does. He's been with Dylan for over a year.

Charlene Dufrayne—Ben's physical therapist.

Hector Alvarez—Hector is one of Alfred's trusted security guards, but he's always around when danger threatens. Is he just good at his job?

Prologue

FBI Special Agent Natasha Rudolph drew her FBI-issued Glock .23 and eyed the burned-out building in a run-down section of downtown Washington, D.C. The broken door hung off its hinges, and as she entered, weapon first, the smell of smoke, urine and dead rats hit her like a noxious wind.

Her wrist communicator beeped quietly.

"Natasha, damn it, where are you?"

It was Storm.

"I just got here," she whispered into her COM unit. "The cell phone signal had to come from this building."

"I'm right behind you. Three minutes. Wait for me."

She knew from experience that in three minutes, Bobby Lee Hutchins could be long gone.

She and fellow Agent Ray Storm had been tracking Hutchins for months, since he'd detonated an explosive device in the Mall in Washington, D.C., that had killed two people and injured over a dozen, including the daughter of a prominent U.S. congressman.

Hutchins was clever, but Natasha and Storm had finally located his mother and tapped her phone. Now they had him, and Natasha wasn't about to let him slip away again.

"Natasha! Answer me!"

After an instant's hesitation, she muted the wrist COM's speaker and stepped into the dim, suffocating interior of the building, her weapon ready.

As she skirted a pile of broken glass, she heard a noise above her head. She froze, tightening her grip on her weapon.

Without moving, she examined the area. She spotted holes in the ceiling, glass and debris on the floor, fire and water damage everywhere.

Carefully, her ears attuned to the smallest sound, she started up the wobbly staircase. Something moved in the darkness beyond the stairs. Natasha jerked, but it was just a mouse. She blew out a breath of relief. She was after human vermin.

Her wrist COM lit up. Storm—trying to reach her again. She ignored it. Hutchins had slipped out of their hands too many times. She wasn't about to lose him this time because protocol dictated she wait for backup. Agents were supposed to use their best discretion in urgent situations.

The sound of wood scraping against wood above her head sent her heart hammering in anticipation.

He was up there. She silently eased her way up the rickety stairs, careful to avoid broken steps. The creak of a board under her boot froze her in place. She stood awkwardly poised between two steps, not daring to breathe. After a few seconds of silence, she moved forward.

As she approached the second floor, she crouched low, taking the steps at a crawl, then slowly raised her head and her gun. Sucking in a deep breath, she prayed Storm really was only seconds away.

She jumped up, swinging her weapon in an arc, checking all sides. *Nothing.*

Cautiously, she angled around the banister.

A soft thump from behind had her wheeling around. A man threw all his weight against her, knocking her to the floor. She twisted as she fell, getting off a shot, but it went wild.

Screaming like a madman, Hutchins swung a rifle barrel at her head. Blinding pain wiped out her vision for an instant. She grasped her Glock desperately.

Then he was over her, the barrel of his rifle digging into her abdomen.

"You shouldn'a gone after my ma!" he screamed.

Natasha pointed her weapon at his chest and struggled to breathe. "Put down the gun!" she gasped.

Hutchins laughed. "You gonna make me?"

"Drop it now or I'll shoot!" Her voice cracked with fear, but she couldn't back down. She didn't want to die. Not today.

He took a step back, and Natasha recognized the instinctive move—he was putting distance between himself and his victim.

"Last chance, Hutchins. Drop it!" she yelled.

His grimy finger tightened on the trigger.

She fired.

Hutchins staggered and blood blossomed on the front of his dirty T-shirt.

She scrambled up, her head spinning.

He recovered and rushed her. Before she could get off another shot, he head-butted her in the gut and her back slammed against the banister. With a loud crack, the railing broke.

Then she was falling—falling. She hit the stairs. Splinters rained around her as her weight broke through the rotten charred wood. Frantically she tried to cushion her landing, but a piece of wood stabbed her hand and her head slammed against a step's solid frame.

A section of floor disintegrated under her weight.

Then with a jarring thud she hit bottom. The impact knocked the breath out of her. A ridge of hard-packed dirt dug into her back.

She looked up. She'd fallen through to the basement. Two floors above, Hutchins raised his rifle. Natasha tried to roll out of his range of vision, but a massive board pinned her legs.

She watched in horrified fascination as his finger tightened on the trigger. She spotted a board she could use as a shield, but she couldn't reach it.

She felt the impact as the bullet slammed into her. The report was deafening. Her stomach lurched at the feel of hot sticky blood pooling in the hollow of her shoulder, and she wondered why it didn't hurt.

Then it did. Pain ripped her in two, stole the last of her breath. Hutchins raised his rifle again. Instinct took over and her fingers tightened on the trigger. She looked down at her hand, surprised she still held the gun.

Gathering the last of her strength, she lifted her arm. Aiming the gun at Hutchins's leering face, she pulled the trigger.

A horrible rumbling filled her ears. Dust and wood and drywall rained down on her. She struggled to move, but her body wouldn't cooperate. The cold dirt beneath her and the heavy, suffocating debris on top of her threatened to crush her. Dust and grit filled her eyes. She couldn't see.

She was trapped. Buried alive.

She screamed and pushed at the jagged boards and piles of drywall and broken glass weighing her down. A sharp edge cut into her palm. Drywall dust coated her throat. Soot caught in her nostrils.

Buried.

Panic threw her into insanity. She screamed until her throat swelled and her mouth was full of soot and dirt. Tears soaked up the dust and caked like concrete on her cheeks.

Terror crowded all rational thought from her brain. The past welled up to suck her into childhood horrors.

She was back in the mangled smoking car, the air thick with the moans of her dying parents, her face and body slick with their blood, her little arms and legs pinned beneath twisted metal.

Her screams mixed with the echo of explosions and gunfire.

But no matter how loud she screamed, nobody came.

Chapter One

Dylan Stryker looked down at his sleeping son. He'd been working with the virtual surgery program and missed Ben's bedtime again.

In the dim glow of a caterpillar night-light, he watched his little boy's lips move slightly with each gentle breath. He looked so small, so innocent—so vulnerable.

Dylan's heart squeezed with guilt and grief and stinging regret. Looking away, his gaze landed on Ben's leg braces in the corner. In stark contrast to his son's softly lit face, the ultralight titanium sucked up the light greedily, shining with the stark whiteness of bones. They mocked him, a constant reminder that his child's handicap was his fault.

Irony twisted his gut. He'd been named a hero for inventing the computer-driven leg supports. Now his own child couldn't walk without them, and it was because of him. He knelt and kissed Ben's cool cheek.

"I love you," he whispered. "I'd die for you if it would change the past."

The bedroom door opened. It was Alfred.

Dylan's senses went on full alert. His chief of security never interrupted him when he was with his son. He slipped quietly through the door to the hall.

"Sorry," Alfred said shortly.

"What is it? Another breach of the fence?" Next week was the third anniversary of the suspicious car crash that had killed his wife and injured his child. The vehicle that had run her off the road had never been found. And despite his and the government's best efforts to cover up Ben's survival, this time each year the tabloids always rehashed the sensationalistic rumors surrounding the crash.

HORROR IN THE HAMPTONS.
. Mad Doctor Hides Hideously
Maimed Son In Airless
Underground Dungeon.

Alfred shook his head at the latest headline, his weathered face grim. "Campbell called me," he said. "We've been hacked."

Dylan cursed. "How bad?"

"In and out within a few seconds, according to Campbell. I should have waited until morning.

Should have let you sleep." Alfred's face was lined with worry.

"No. I wasn't asleep. I need to know as soon as anything happens."

"What for? So you have something else on your mind to keep you from sleeping? You couldn't have stopped the hacker."

Dylan headed for the back stairs. "I could have tried."

Alfred followed, laying a hand on Dylan's arm. "He's gone now. Go back to Ben. Try to get some sleep."

"I can't sleep. You know that. I might as well work." Dylan rubbed his burning eyes.

"Son, this is almost certainly a domestic terrorist cell. Why don't you take NSA up on their offer of protection?"

Dylan sighed. "I talked to them today."

"You've decided to move to a secure location?" Hope tinged Alfred's gravelly voice. As proud as the ex-military man was of his security measures, he'd made it clear that he'd prefer having Dylan and Ben under the government protection.

Dylan shook his head and rubbed the back of his neck. "We've had this conversation. I'm not sending Ben away. And I can't go with him. The interface hardware is at a critical point—too delicate to be moved, and we're still debugging the software. I can't afford to lose even a couple of days…." He heard the desperation in his own voice. Alfred knew as well as he did the real reason he was working night and day.

Time was running out for Ben.

"So why'd you call NSA?"

"I told them that if they want their damn super-soldier technology, they'll find me the best computer expert in the country. They promised me someone within forty-eight hours."

SPECIAL AGENT Natasha Rudolph wiped her palms down her slacks as the doors slid shut, locking her in an elevator that was about to take her underground. Mitch Decker, Special Agent in Charge, had warned her this assignment would be difficult.

However, he hadn't mentioned that the computer lab where she'd be working was twelve feet belowground on a secluded estate in the Hamptons. She closed her eyes as the elevator started downward.

"Agent Rudolph?"

She opened her eyes to find the military type who'd met her at the front door eyeing her hands. She realized she was clenching her fists.

"Yes? Mintz, isn't it?" She deliberately relaxed her fingers. "I'm fine. Looking forward to getting started. It's been a long day." She bit her lip. She sounded like a babbling idiot. She set her jaw and silently commanded her heart to stop fluttering and her hands to stay serenely at her sides.

Alfred Mintz frowned at her as the elevator doors slid silently open.

She wiped her palms again, and stepped out into a brightly lit hall. It looked as if all the walls were made of glass. Natasha swallowed nervously. Not very substantial. She resisted the urge to glance up at the ceiling. How did these walls hold up the tons of dirt and steel above their heads?

Ignoring the burning sensation on her scalp that signaled rising panic, she concentrated on staying calm.

Mintz started down the hall, leaving her to catch up. "You may not get to meet Dr. Stryker tonight. If he's in the virtual surgery lab, we won't disturb him."

They passed empty offices, furnished cubicles with computer workstations, and a door labeled Restroom And Showers that thankfully was not walled with glass.

"I thought he was anxious for me to get started reinforcing the firewall," she said.

Just past the restroom was a longer, solid glass wall. She saw a dim glow through the glass, although the glare of the brighter hall lights kept her from seeing inside the room clearly. She had the impression of chrome and steel.

Mintz stopped at the door. He nodded, his gaze on something or someone beyond the glass.

Natasha shaded her eyes and squinted. The room was an exercise room—a very well-equipped exercise room.

And as she watched, a very well-equipped man stepped off a treadmill and grabbed a towel.

A few seconds later, the man stepped through the glass door and walked toward her with loose-limbed grace. He wore a gray T-shirt and gray exercise pants. The T-shirt was dark with sweat, and hugged the planes of his chest and shoulders. Its tail hung loose, hinting at a flat, ridged belly. The pants fit snugly over his lean hips and long legs.

His biceps flexed as he toweled his face and hair, then slung the towel around his neck.

Natasha gaped at him. Who was he? Not Stryker, surely. This guy did not look like a famous neurosurgeon. Maybe he was the young bioengineer she'd been told was building the interface implant—Jerry Campbell.

Mintz stepped aside as he approached.

When Natasha pulled her gaze away from his sweaty, sexy body and met his gaze, the lines around his red-rimmed blue eyes and the exhaustion on his face came into focus.

This was no kid. But, who—

His sharp blue eyes burned into hers.

"Dylan Stryker, this is Special Agent Natasha Rudolph," Mintz said.

"Ah, yes. NSA said you'd be here by this evening," Stryker said wryly, lifting one brow.

It was him. "Well, NSA and the FBI tend to respond more favorably to requests than demands."

"I don't have time to wait for the bureaucracy to process a request."

His gaze flickered down her body and back up. Then he held out his hand. "So *you're* the best hacker-buster in the known universe."

She stared at the elegantly long, blunt-tipped fingers and neatly trimmed nails. His hands were the only thing about him that fit the information she'd been given. They looked like surgeon's hands.

The only recent photos of him were long-range, grainy tabloid shots. From them she'd gotten the impression of a thin, hatchet-faced, obsessed scientist.

Boy was she wrong!

"Hacker-buster?" She shook her head. "No. Computer expert." Her voice was steadier than her insides.

This was Dylan Stryker. Her head spun as lurid headlines filled her vision.

HORROR IN THE HAMPTONS.
Mad Doctor Hides Hideously
Maimed Son In Airless
Underground Dungeon.

It was typical tabloid fare and it made her shudder each time she thought about it, made her dread meeting Stryker's child, whom Decker had told her was paralyzed. How could anyone keep a child in this place? *Underground dungeon— underground lab.* Close enough.

"Dr. Stryker." She took his extended hand, and his intensity hit her like the back draft from a fire. Shock and awareness skittered along her spine. His grasp was firm and brief, leaving her palm feeling singed by his touch.

"So, Agent Rudolph, are you really the best?" His voice held a challenge.

"Yes, I am," she said without hesitation.

His straight mouth tilted slightly at one corner. "Good. Perfect."

He nodded, dislodging a trickle of sweat that slid down over his temple and down his jawbone.

He glanced at his watch, used the towel on his damp hair again, then turned to Mintz. "Get her settled and put her to work. What about equipment?"

"Brought it with her. Where do you want her?"

"In the office across from the virtual surgery lab." He pointed farther down the hall. Then he looked at her. "How much equipment do you have?"

"I'd rather have an office upstairs—" Natasha started, but Mintz was listing her equipment for Stryker. Neither one of them paid any attention to her.

"Is there anything else you need, Agent Rudolph?"

Windows. Lots of windows. "Any chance I could work upstairs somewhere?"

"No. Out of the question." Stryker eyed her suspiciously. "Are you sure you can handle this job?"

"Yes, of course," she said, thankful her voice was still steady. She had a job to do. And that meant forgetting that there were truckloads of dirt and an entire mansion over her head. Her career was on the line. She had to succeed—windows or no windows.

"I assume I can start right away." The quicker she got started, the quicker she could expose the hacker and get out of this hole in the ground.

"Alfred'll take care of anything you need," Stryker said with a wave of his hand.

As he turned away, his gaze met hers in a fleeting, intense glance that seared her to the bone. His clear blue eyes burned as brightly as an oxygen flame, warming her cheeks and stirring a cauldron of unexpected emotions within her.

He might be tired and unkempt, underfed and distracted, but Dylan Stryker exuded an air of command and—she searched for the right word… *masculinity*…that hummed through her like the ring of a perfectly pitched tuning fork. She blinked and dropped her gaze.

"Thanks, Alfred." Stryker headed back to his lab.

Natasha felt stunned. According to his file, Stryker was thirty-three, and already known worldwide for his breakthroughs with computer-assisted mobility in nerve-damaged patients.

Natasha had studied everything the FBI had on him, including clippings from the tabloids. He'd been thirty when his wife was killed three years before.

It has long been rumored that Stryker's infant son did not die in the mysterious car crash that killed his wife….

Natasha stared at Stryker's broad shoulders and lean hips until she realized Mintz had left her behind again. She hurried to catch up. He used his thumbprint and keyed in digits from a pass code generator. The door clicked open to reveal a small foyer banked with elevators.

"Where are we going? I need to start work."

Mintz punched the call button. "I'll show you to your room first, so you can freshen up. Have you eaten?"

She nodded, finding it difficult to pull her thoughts away from Dylan Stryker. He was so completely different from her expectations. He was driven, maybe even obsessed. But there was something else about him. Something dark and haunted lurked behind his brilliant blue eyes.

"I assume you've been fully briefed on our situation?" Mintz asked.

"Yes, sir. I'm here to stop a hacker and construct a firewall. And of course, to help with physical security."

Mintz shook his head. "Physical security is not your job. Two of your fellow agents are on the outside to help my staff handle that. You concentrate on the computer."

Irritation stiffened her shoulders. "I've studied the aerial photos. You've done a good job of camouflaging the house."

Too good for her taste. This was her first assignment since her injury. And now she understood why Decker had given her a choice. He'd told her that the staff psychiatrist had declared her *minimally* qualified. At the time she was furious, and eager to prove the shrink wrong.

Now she got it. How ironic that this job tapped into her worst fears. Before her injury, this would have been just another assignment, and her mild claustrophobia would be manageable. But now she was fighting for her career. If she couldn't conquer her irrational fear of closed spaces, she'd lose her job.

She suppressed a shudder, drew in a lungful of conditioned air and repeated the mantra Dr. Shay had given her to calm her panic.

Quiet and safe. Plenty of fresh air. Breathe. Breathe. Breathe.

It was nighttime now, but she knew from the photos Decker had shown her that even during the day, the massive house was shrouded in darkness. "I saw the infrared photos. How do you keep from broadcasting body heat?"

"The canopy that stretches over the entire house is made of a specially designed heat-repelling mesh," Mintz answered. "Some sunlight does get in. But it's very good camouflage."

"Right. The perfect hiding place," she said wryly.

"Not perfect," Mintz responded. "We do what we can to quash any rumors that this is Dylan's base of operations. But occasionally somebody tries to breach the walls, or flies over in a helicopter. Usually paparazzi."

The faint note of disapproval in his voice intrigued her. She looked at him, but his stern face gave away nothing.

The elevator doors opened and they stepped inside.

"And now it looks like we've got a hacker."

"Did I understand that your computer guy said he got in and out clean?"

He nodded. "Jerry Campbell. He's the bioengineer working with Dylan. He assured us the hacker left nothing behind."

"Bioengineer? Who's handling the computer system?"

Mintz cleared his throat impatiently. "Dr. Stryker wants as few people involved as possible."

"I don't know how good a bioengineer he is but he's wrong about the hackers. They always leave something," Natasha said firmly. "I need to talk with him, find out what he saw."

"Tomorrow."

"Why not tonight? What he tells me will help determine what other equipment I'll need."

Mintz shook his head. "He's busy with Dylan tonight."

"Well, maybe when he takes a *break*," she said impatiently. She needed to get finished and get out. The assignment was already giving her the creeps.

The FBI shrink's evaluation taunted her. Hasn't fully dealt with her claustrophobia. She had to defeat the feeling of losing control if she was going to succeed.

"Believe me, Agent Rudolph. We're anxious for you to get started. Get the equipment you brought set up tonight. Assess the system. Decide what else you need. Then first thing tomorrow, you can meet Campbell and have him brief you on the hacker's movements."

Natasha started to press him, but he held up his hand.

"Dylan's at a critical point in the debugging process right now. I'm surprised he stopped long enough to exercise, although with the amount of tension he's carrying around…" Mintz set his jaw. "He needs you, but he resents the time it's going to take to bring you up to speed. Time is the one thing he doesn't have. If you're as good as your superiors say you are, he'll figure it out soon enough."

She tried one last frontal attack. "NSA is *extremely* anxious to get their hands on that interface."

"NSA is not Dylan's primary concern."

Before she could ponder that comment, the elevator doors slid open, and they stepped out into the atrium through which she'd entered. It was laid out in brightly veined Italian marble. A mezzanine lined with bookshelves bisected the walls.

The high ceiling was crowned by a massive domed skylight. Although the sun had set, a pink and purple glow filtered through the glass dome.

"I assume the skylight is shielded, too?"

Mintz glanced up. "Yep. The mesh doesn't block the moon and stars as much as it does the sun. And there's clear plastic sheeting to keep out the rain while allowing a little sunlight in."

The vise that had squeezed her chest since she got here loosened a bit. She took a long cleansing breath. At least she could see the sky—sort of.

Mintz gave her a quick rundown of the house's layout. He pointed to the front doors. "That's north. The staff quarters are on the east. The kitchen, the patio and Ben's play area are that way." He pointed southward. "And the west door goes to the family quarters. Your suite is in there, next to Ben's."

As he finished, a metallic thumping echoed in her ears.

"Alfred!" A toddler ran in from the kitchen area.

"This is Ben." Mintz's controlled drill-sergeant face creased in a smile.

Natasha's heart twisted in compassion as the

little boy ran clumsily toward Mintz. The metallic thumps were caused by bright silver braces that crisscrossed his little legs like an erector set. Beneath the clanking of the braces, she heard the almost silent whirr of a motor.

"Alfred!" Ben shouted. "Where's my daddy?"

He was the image of his father—black hair, blue eyes. He didn't seem to notice the braces that encumbered him.

The tabloid stories held a kernel of truth, but they were totally wrong about the child. Ben wasn't pathetically crippled. He was bright and energetic. Still, a horrific vision haunted her—a crumpled, crushed vehicle with a baby trapped inside, crying for his mother.

She shuddered and her breath hitched.

"Agent Rudolph, are you all right?"

She forced herself to breathe evenly. "Of course."

Ben tugged on Mintz's hand. "Is Daddy coming?"

"Pardner, why aren't you in bed?" Mintz said in a surprisingly gentle voice.

"I'm waiting for my daddy."

"Where's Miss Charlene?" Mintz inclined his head toward Natasha. "Ben's physical therapist."

Ben's face began to crumple. "Not Charlene. Daddy. He can take me outside to see the moon." Tears shimmered on his long lashes.

As Natasha watched in astonishment, the grizzled security chief lifted Ben. The boy wrapped his arms around Mintz's neck and tucked his face into his collar.

"Your daddy's working tonight. I want you to meet someone."

Ben turned his head so that one dark blue eye was visible. "No." He hid his face again. "I want my daddy."

"This is Natasha. Can you say Natasha?"

Ben shook his head, but curiosity got the better of him and he peeked sideways at her. "Tasha?"

His little voice saying the nickname she hadn't heard since childhood caused her to smile, even as it cut into her heart.

"Hi, Ben." She'd never been around kids, so the ache in her chest and the tightness in her throat surprised her. He was so sweet and so vulnerable and brave. And he'd transformed Stryker's gruff, rigid security chief into a doting grandfather.

"Come on, Ben. Let's get you tucked in."

Ben still peered at her sidelong, from the folds of Mintz's shirt. "Tasha come, too?"

"Oh, no. I don't—"

"Sure Natasha can come, too," Mintz said. "And later, your daddy'll come in to say good-night."

Ben shifted and sat up straight, confident in Mintz's protective embrace.

"Go this way, Tasha." He pointed as Mintz headed for the west hall. He watched her over Mintz's shoulder.

What should she say? She had no clue how to talk to a kid. "How old are you, Ben?"

He held up three pudgy fingers. "Three and a half."

Of course. A pang of sadness hit her square in the chest. The car crash had occurred this time of year—September—three years ago. Ben had been six months old, too young to remember the crash or the pain or the sound of his mother dying. *Thank God.*

They entered Ben's room to find a young woman with shiny brown hair folding back the covers on his bed.

"This is Charlene Dufrayne," Mintz said. "Charlene, Special Agent Natasha Rudolph."

"Oh, the computer expert." Charlene gave Natasha a wary nod as she took Ben from Mintz. "We've all heard about you."

Natasha rapidly cataloged the other woman's appearance. Medium height, late twenties, pretty. In good shape. She'd be good for Ben.

She glanced around the child's room. It was painted a bright blue, and filled with every toy a little boy could want. But something about it sent an eerie shiver through her.

"Okay, cowboy, let's get you ready for bed," Charlene said, setting him on his bed.

"I stay awake 'til Daddy comes."

"Daddy may not come tonight. He's very busy."

As Ben's eager face fell, Natasha's heart ached. Charlene began to unlock the braces.

Mintz opened a connecting door and gestured for Natasha to precede him into the next room.

She stepped through the door, her gaze still lingering on Ben's room. As Mintz turned on the lights and she looked around the starkly decorated room, it hit her what was bothering her.

"These rooms don't have any windows," she croaked. Her throat constricted.

"This is the only level of the house above-ground. That makes it vulnerable. Windows would greatly increase that vulnerability."

Her pulse jumped as she pushed away the panic and forced herself to nod. "Vulnerability. Of course. That... makes sense."

As an FBI agent, she understood, but no amount of rational thinking stilled her knee-jerk response to the vaultlike rooms. This was why she'd scrimped and saved until she could afford a top-floor condo in Washington, D.C., where all her walls were glass, and the sun streamed in every day.

She couldn't get Ben's sweet little face out of

her mind. It horrified her to think he'd lived his whole life locked inside these walls.

"Is there a problem, Agent Rudolph?" Mintz's voice was edged with ice.

She quoted her mantra for dealing with panic. *Quiet and safe. Plenty of fresh air. Breathe. Breathe. Breathe.*

"No, sir. I realize safety is your primary concern. It's just that Ben is—" She swallowed. "He's a growing boy. He needs sunshine and—" she faltered when Mintz glowered at her "—fresh air."

"Ben's needs are not your purview."

She lifted her chin. "So far, apparently nothing is my purview. You've vetoed every suggestion I've made. I must say, your trust in me is underwhelming."

"Not just you," he muttered, his face grim. "Anyone." He faced her. "Understand this, Agent Rudolph. As far as the public knows, Ben died in the car crash that killed his mother. Dylan has gone to superhuman lengths to keep the boy here with him."

She searched his face. "You don't approve."

The lines in his face deepened. "I built this place to withstand an explosion the magnitude of Oklahoma City. But nobody can guard against human ingenuity. All it'll take is one person breaching the walls, or hacking into the computers. NSA wants Dylan and his interface safe. They've offered to place him and Ben in a secure government location."

"And you want that, too." No matter how protected the estate was, the child could still be in danger. Still, now that she'd met Ben, she understood why his father refused to let him out of his sight. After only a few minutes, his innocent, angelic face had already made a dent in her heart.

"What I want is not relevant. Ben is Dylan's son. He would give up everything for him, even his own life."

"I get the feeling you'd do the same for either of them."

Mintz averted his gaze as he dug in his pocket and handed her a small digital device. He cleared his throat. "Your fingerprints are already in the security system. This is your pass code generator. You'll want to keep it on your person at all times. The code changes every forty-five seconds. Your print on the keypad plus the entry of this code will unlock any door on the estate. There will *not* be any security issues, understood?"

Natasha stiffened. "Understood, sir." She took the device.

"I'll be back in an hour to take you down to the lab."

"I can find my way—" she started, but he'd turned on his heel and left. The door closed silently behind him.

She sat down on the bed and closed her eyes, thankful to be alone for a few moments. Her neck and shoulders ached from maintaining her composure. Now, as she flexed them, her entire body began to tremble.

Underground laboratory. Windowless rooms. No wonder Decker had worried about her ability to handle this assignment. She felt the weight of the house and the closeness of the impenetrable walls. Her lungs sucked in air greedily.

After twenty-two years, she'd thought she'd conquered her worst personal demon, until Bobby Lee Hutchins had buried her alive.

Horror slithered along her nerve endings as she recalled the endless dark. She'd been certain her life was over.

But her partner Storm hadn't given up. He'd stayed there while the workers cleared away boards and drywall and dirt. He'd kept calling out to her even though she didn't have enough breath to answer him.

When they got her to the hospital she had four cracked ribs, a collapsed lung and a broken leg, none of which bothered her as much as the hours of terror she'd spent buried under the debris.

She'd experienced the worst. This job should be a piece of cake. All she had to do was keep her cool for a few days until they caught the hacker.

She took a deep breath of artificially cooled air and reminded herself that she wasn't buried. She was on the top level—aboveground. The air smelled fresh and the room was large and clean. There was no reason to feel claustrophobic.

She closed her eyes, but it didn't help. Her demon was back. The walls were closing in.

THE HACKER grinned as his fingers flew over the keyboard. Just a few more keystrokes and he'd have his first look at Dr. Dylan Stryker's neural interface operating software.

He'd been working toward this moment for three years, since the botched kidnapping of Stryker's wife and son. He'd learned a lot from the extremists who had run the neurosurgeon's wife and baby son off the road.

Idiots. Their blind devotion to their cause came in handy, but only if they had a leader to guide them. *He* was in control this time. There would be no mistakes.

There was nothing more satisfying than to beat the government at their own game. He'd waited a long time for another chance to prove his superiority.

Eight years ago, he'd not only cracked the FBI's domestic terrorist database, he'd framed a young hacker for the breach. He'd needed to get rid of her—she'd been too good.

By planting subtle but identifiable clues inside the FBI's computer program, he'd led lead investigators to the computer lab at the college she attended. Once they'd identified the computer, it was simple to trace her ID and find the evidence he'd so carefully planted.

His brilliant frame-up had made him famous in the hacking world. And now he was back. The National Security Agency had designed Stryker's firewall, and it was impressive. But so were his skills.

Alert to any sign of detection, he typed a few lines of code, nudging the protective barrier around the software that could make the fabled computer-enhanced supersoldier a reality.

A sense of omnipotence streaked through him. His fingertips tingled and a visceral exhilaration sizzled in his groin. Nobody except another hacker could understand the feeling.

All he needed was a few seconds to gain entrance to the ultrasecure area where Stryker's files and programs on the neural interface were stored.

He was typing the last bit of code when his cell phone rang.

He jumped. "Son of a—" He jabbed the talk button. "*What?* I'm in the middle of something."

"The computer expert is here."

Excitement spread through him like electricity. At last, a challenge. "When?"

"An hour or so ago. She's an FBI agent— Natasha something."

"Natasha?" His fingers went numb with shock. "Are you sure?" He stood, propelling the computer chair backward. "What does she look like?"

"Tall. Long blond hair. Do you know her?"

Natasha. "Of course not." Sweat prickled his neck and armpits. He glanced at his computer screen. "Is she online?"

"No. She's in her room."

"Did she have a laptop?"

"Nope. Mintz won't allow wireless in here."

"I want to know the instant she puts her fingers on the keyboard."

"I'll try. You know how hard it is to call out. How much longer until—"

"Don't start with me. I've got to think. You just make sure you're ready."

"Are you sure I'll be safe?"

"God, just do your job and give me a break." He jabbed the disconnect button.

Tall. Blonde. Rage burned through him.

That was his luck. Of course they would send

Natasha. His nemesis. The only hacker he'd ever known who could even approach his talent. He'd realized her worth the first time he'd ever met her.

He sat and pulled the keyboard toward him. He cracked his knuckles and flexed his fingers, then arched his neck. A slow smile spread over his features. In a way it was like a karmic balance.

He'd almost destroyed her once because she refused to follow his lead, but fate in the guise of the FBI had intervened. They'd trained her and hired her instead of sending her to prison. At the time the irony had eaten a hole in his gut.

Now he understood. His patience, his efforts to distance himself from the radical group who'd caused the death of Stryker's wife, were paying off in a way he'd never dreamed.

Stryker's interface and the software that operated it were worth billions. Several foreign leaders were waiting, cash in hand, for the technology that had the potential to create a real supersoldier.

Yes, he wanted the money, but that wasn't why he was doing this.

He finally had a chance to prove once and for all that he was the best. He was pitted against Natasha Rudolph again.

He held the advantage because he knew her greatest fear. Before this was over, she'd pay for dodging prison eight years ago. And her punishment this time would be worse—so much worse.

He put on his telephone headset and hit a preset number on his cell. He had to make sure everything was in place for his first destructive attack on Stryker's estate.

As he waited he placed his fingertips on the keyboard. A thrill, almost sexual, shot through him, all the way to his groin. *Natasha* was on the other end of his computer.

It would double his pleasure to know she would die along with Stryker.

Chapter Two

By midnight, Natasha was certain of two things. Someone had definitely targeted Dylan's computer, and she needed much more powerful equipment if she was going to build an effective firewall.

She stretched and arched her neck to loosen the tight muscles, then glanced toward the ceiling. If she had to be down here much longer, she'd go crazy. Sure the lab was brilliantly lit and air-conditioned, but that didn't change the fact that it was buried under twelve feet of dirt, steel and wood.

A movement across the hall caught her eye. Dylan Stryker leaned back in his chair and rubbed his face. He'd appeared in the glass-walled room across from hers a couple of hours before, freshly showered and dressed in neat khaki slacks and a navy polo shirt that left his long, muscled arms bare.

Even though she'd been concentrating on the patterns in screen after screen of code, a part of her had remained acutely aware of his presence.

Mintz had told her he was working on a computerized surgical simulation program. It had only taken a few seconds' observation for her to figure out that he was using a stylus like a surgical tool to practice attaching microscopic nerves to microscopic wires. *The neural interface.*

She'd read the basics of the device in a classified NSA memo. It was a rectangular box about the size of a USB plug, maybe a centimeter long. The 3-D computer-generated mock-up looked like a millipede with thousands of hairlike microfibers covering its surface. Once the device was surgically implanted into a human being, and each microfiber was attached to the proper neural sheath, the interface would feed impulses to and from nerves too damaged to receive proper signals from the brain.

No wonder the government wanted it. The possible uses were astounding. The supersoldier of fiction, with computer-enhanced reflexes, sharpened vision and hearing, perfectly timed response and accuracy, could become a reality. The thought of that technology falling into the hands of terrorists was horrifying.

Abruptly, Dylan pushed back from his workstation and stood. He pushed his hands through his hair and started to pace.

Campbell, sitting at the other workstation,

yawned and said something. Dylan shook his head and shrugged his shoulders, as if trying to work the tension from his body.

His movements were spare and graceful. As he rubbed his neck, his biceps flexed and he arched his back, emphasizing the seductive curve at the base of his spine and his strong, well-shaped buttocks.

He turned toward her. Embarrassed, she dropped her gaze to the flat-screen monitor. Studying his physical attributes wasn't getting her any closer to the hacker.

She reexamined the section of code that had grabbed her attention earlier, and suddenly the jumble of numbers and letters coalesced into a pattern.

"Why you clever little—" she whispered to the unknown hacker as she advanced to the next screen, searching for the same telltale string of numbers she'd just spotted.

Whoever he was, he was good. As she'd told Mintz, they always left something behind, but this guy's tag was almost undetectable.

It was also vaguely familiar. She frowned at the tiny string of code. She'd seen that pattern before. A nauseating dread began to build in her stomach. Could it be Tom?

No. That would be too weird a coincidence. Although… he had always been fascinated with the fringe groups who would do anything to bring down the government. Not because *he* had anything against the U.S.

He loved being in control, and he'd always said the zealots who would die for their cause were ridiculously easy to manipulate.

Her heart jackhammered in her throat. If it *was* Tom, did he know she was here? Eight years ago he'd framed her for hacking into the FBI's domestic terrorist database. But eight years ago she'd been naive and trusting. She was smarter now. Of course, Tom probably was, too.

Her peripheral vision picked up a movement to her left. She stiffened and casually dropped her hand to the fanny pack where she kept her weapon.

"What's so interesting on that screen?"

It was Dylan. She glanced up at him, then through the glass toward the lab. She'd been caught off guard. Something that never happened to her.

"No," he said, his eyes twinkling. "I can't walk through walls. Alfred believes in triple redundancy. There are doors all over the place." A ghost of a smile flickered about his mouth, making him look younger and achingly handsome.

"Triple redundancy is a good thing." Having plenty of doors was even better—excellent in fact. She hoped they all led upstairs.

Dylan studied the young woman the FBI

claimed was the best hacker-tracker they had. She was young, but computer expertise didn't depend on years of training. The best hackers were often under twenty-five.

He put his hand on the back of her chair and leaned over, studying her screen. "Find something?"

Her pale blond hair tickled his nose, and the scent of springtime and wild strawberries filled his nostrils. He took a deep breath, faintly shocked at his reaction. He had a sudden urge to run his fingers through her silky hair, to nuzzle the graceful curve of her neck.

What the hell was he thinking?

She cleared her throat and pulled slightly away from him. "I've found traces of the hacker."

He squeezed his eyes shut for an instant, trying to throw off his body's instantaneous response to her closeness. He straightened.

"You told Alfred the hacker couldn't have gotten out clean."

She shook her head. "That's right. Everything that's done on a computer leaves a trace. This guy is very good, but—"

"You found him." Dylan leaned in close to the monitor again, curious about what she'd seen. At that moment she turned her head. Her brilliant green eyes were only a couple of inches away from his, her mouth so close he felt her breath.

Her eyes widened and she turned her head back to the screen.

"In less than three hours."

"I—I haven't found him, just his trail."

She nervously moistened her lips and a spear of lust streaked through him.

As if she knew the effect she was having on him, she leaned farther back in her chair and took a deep breath. "Is this your first hacking attempt?"

For his own sake, he straightened and stepped away from her. He crossed his arms. "We get reports of failed attempts—maybe once or twice a month. But two days ago Campbell received an alert. It wasn't just a knock at the door. It was unauthorized access."

"Well, either Campbell made another mistake or this is a different hacker, because *this* guy's been accessing the vulnerable areas of your system for at least two years."

Dylan stared at her. "Two years?" He shook his head in disbelief. "That's impossible!"

She sent him a sharp look.

"Okay. Two years." His insides twisted in horror. He ran his hand across the back of his neck, massaging the tight muscles there. *Two years. Ben!*

"What kind of damage has he done?"

"He's accessed your document files, household calendars and schedules, financial records, buying habits."

Dylan's jaw clenched and a cold fear engulfed him. "Buying habits. Household calendars." He cursed vividly. "Then he knows Ben is alive. What else does he know?"

"Anything that came in or went out via e-mail."

"Even to or from NSA?"

"That's right."

"Damn it!" He whirled and slammed his palm into the door facing.

Natasha jumped.

"Sorry," he said, glancing at her sheepishly. He rubbed his hand. "So he knows about the interface. Knows how close I am to perfecting it." Fear and rage swirled through him.

"What the hell good is a firewall then? What's the point of all the damned computer security if—?"

She held up a hand. "He hasn't cracked the encryption that protects your neural interface. Not yet anyway."

He blew out a breath. "Thank God for that. But why hasn't my software detected him? It was developed by NSA."

Natasha smiled without humor. "That's why he hasn't gotten what he wants. But whoever he is, he's that good. Firewalls are built by people. People can crack them."

The confidence in her voice intrigued him. Dylan eyed her. She could pass for a college kid. Too young, too innocent, to be so sure of herself. He asked her a question he already knew the answer to. "Could *you* have gotten into my system?"

Natasha stared into Dylan's eyes, into the lake of blue fire that burned so intensely. She resisted the urge to look away. "Yes."

He nodded as he studied her thoughtfully. "So are you a hacker?"

She swallowed. "No." *Not anymore.*

His gaze searched her face. Did he believe her?

"Okay then, who is this guy?" he asked.

The sixty-four-thousand-dollar question. She looked at the screen and didn't quite lie this time. "I'm pretty sure I've seen him before. Since I've been with the FBI, I've run across a lot of very good hackers. This is almost certainly one of them. But to catch him, I'm going to need much better equipment."

"Fine. I'll contact NSA."

"No need. My boss can have it here sometime early tomorrow by jet courier."

"Good. Do it."

She began to breathe easier. He'd been satisfied with her answer about the hacker's ID. There was no way she was going to tell anyone of her suspicion that the hacker was Tom. Not until she was sure, and maybe not even then. She told herself no one needed to know she'd been so desperate for money to pay for college that she'd performed hacking jobs for the same man who might be attacking Dylan's system—who might even be responsible for the death of his wife and the crippling of his young son.

A sickening dread spread through her, and her gut clenched.

Dylan propped a hip on the edge of her desk, way too close for comfort. His eyes blazed.

"Well, Agent Rudolph, you are good. I assume you're old enough to be an FBI agent. What are you—twenty-five? Twenty-six."

"I'm twenty-seven, and my name is Natasha."

"How did you get to be the government's best hacker-buster?"

She smiled wryly. "So you're still not sure about me?"

His cheeks turned faintly pink. "It's not that I question your ability—"

"You just question my ability," she tossed back at him.

His long black lashes floated down for an instant, giving her his answer.

Normally, she couldn't care less if some military type or stiff-necked suit doubted her expertise. But the fact that Dylan had reservations about her made her feel as if she had something to prove. She pushed that notion aside. She wasn't here to impress him, just to do her job and get out as soon as possible.

"Let's just say I had a lot of incentive," she said wryly. Incentive. That was an understatement. Mitch Decker had saved her from going to prison for hacking into classified files. No matter that she'd been framed. Prison was prison. She owed a big debt to the U.S. government.

Dylan's dark brows went up. "Incentive?"

She gnawed on her lower lip. His intensity was mesmerizing and a little frightening. When he looked at her, she felt as if she were the only person in his world. She dropped her gaze to her hands. She wasn't answering any more questions.

"I need to contact Mitch and give him my equipment list. Until it gets here there's not much I can do, unless you give me access to your program files."

Dylan shook his head and stood.

"Look, Dr. Stryker. If I'm going to do my job—"

He broke in. "It's almost midnight. You should be in bed."

She tilted her head at him. "As you just pointed out, I'm well over twenty-one, all grown-up. I usually make my own decisions about bed."

She hadn't meant it to come out like that. To

her dismay, she felt a flush rising from her neck to her cheeks.

The corner of his mouth turned up. He took a step backward and leaned against the door facing.

"Campbell's working on the programming code right now. You should get a good night's sleep and get started in the morning."

"Yes, sir," she snapped, and came to her feet.

Even slouched wearily against the door facing, he commanded attention. His shirt strained over his biceps and lay gently against his well-defined abs.

He exuded strength, competence, and yes—obsession. Not to mention undeniable sexuality. She'd never been in the presence of anyone so physically compelling.

He gave her a quick nod, straightened and turned on his heel. "I assume you can find your way to your room, being so grown-up and all," he said over his shoulder.

JERRY CAMPBELL yawned loudly and twisted his stringy hair back into its ponytail. He'd stared at screen after screen of computer code until he was cross-eyed. It was almost midnight. Dr. Stryker had told him to go to bed an hour ago. He was about ready to take that advice.

But first—he glanced through the glass walls of

the virtual surgery lab, searching the halls and other offices, making sure no one was around. Typing briskly, he opened his e-mail account and composed a message, quickly attached a file and pressed Send. Then he began to shut down the computer.

THE WALLS WERE CLOSING IN. Little Tasha pushed against the car seat that pinned her. But she couldn't move. She tried not to think about the blood, or why her mama and daddy wouldn't talk to her.

A big boom shook the car. She shrieked. That one was louder than the first, the one that had smashed the front of the car.

She saw a flash of light, and then another boom rumbled through her. She couldn't see! Couldn't breathe!

Daddy!

Natasha sat up, gasping for air.

Her chest heaved as spasms racked her rigid muscles. Her mind crashed back into her body. She'd been dreaming. Again.

Where was she? Not in the car where her parents had died. Not buried under mountains of debris in a burned-out building.

She was inside Dylan Stryker's secluded estate—in the windowless pitch-dark room. No wonder she'd dreamed of being trapped.

Quiet and safe. Plenty of fresh air. Breathe. Breathe. Breathe.

She kicked at the tangled sheets. She had to get out of there. She'd go sit under the skylight.

As she stood up, she heard something. It sounded as if it was just outside her door. Silently, she slipped her Glock from under her pillow and slid out of bed, gliding silently along the wall, listening. As she neared the door, she saw the knob slowly turn. The door swung open a few inches, until a pale night-light from the hall sent a long shadow across the floor near the foot of her bed.

Natasha flattened herself against the wall, her eyes glued to the hand on the knob. She braced herself, then grabbed the wrist with her left hand and yanked, aiming her weapon at the intruder's neck.

"Don't move," she hissed, her heart hammering.

A deafening screech split the air. Natasha jerked and almost dropped her gun.

Sirens.

Shaking her head, gripping her gun until her hand ached, she shoved the intruder back through the door and against the wall of the hallway.

A small, feminine grunt reached her ears, almost drowned out by the earsplitting screech.

It was Charlene. Natasha flipped her around to face her, but she didn't lower her gun. "What were you doing?"

Charlene's eyes were wide with panic. "The sirens. I knew you wouldn't know what they were. The first time I heard them I nearly jumped out of my skin." She laughed nervously.

Natasha stared at the woman for a beat, and frowned. Had the sirens awoken her?

Just then, Ben's door opened. Dylan came out, his hair tousled and his trousers wrinkled. He was shirtless and barefoot. He clutched his polo shirt in one hand and his loafers in the other. His sleepy eyes were too bright, burning with azure fire.

"Charlene, get in there with Ben. Natasha, go back to your room." He dropped his shoes to the floor and slipped into them.

Charlene scooted around Natasha, past Dylan and through the door to Ben's room.

"What's happening?" Natasha yelled over the siren's screech.

Dylan glared at her. He opened his mouth, but she didn't give him a chance to speak. She darted back inside her room for her gear. She grabbed her hiking boots, a black pullover and her leather fanny pack.

As she stepped back into the hall, the sirens finally decreased in volume and faded.

Dylan hadn't bothered to wait for her. He'd already reached the end of the hall.

She stuffed her weapon into the fanny pack along with her badge and the pass code generator, then hopped on one foot at a time as she pulled on her boots. She caught up to him when he paused to put on his shirt.

His bare, shadowed shoulders rippled and gleamed in the low light as he tugged the polo shirt over his head.

It was impossible to ignore the yearning that had taken root inside her when he'd appeared without his shirt—the yearning to touch his hot, smooth skin.

She didn't like the way he affected her. It was distracting—and dangerous.

"What are those sirens?" she asked.

He vaulted down the stairs. She was right behind him. "Security breach."

"Breach? Where?"

"This way. The west side." Dylan opened the exit door at the foot of the stairs. Campbell burst into the stairwell from the lab.

"What are you doing still down here?" Dylan frowned at his bioengineer. Campbell looked as though he'd been in a tussle. His long hair was tangled and loose around his face. He pushed it back with hands that shook.

"I was shutting down the computers when the sirens went off. Scared the crap out of me."

"It's after four. I thought you were going to bed hours ago."

Dylan held the exit door for Campbell and Natasha. As she passed him, she met his gaze with a narrow, questioning look. Was she also wondering why Campbell looked as though he'd just crawled through a fence?

"I lost track of time," Campbell said. "Where's the breach?"

"Spotlights," Natasha said, pointing west. She took off toward them at a jog.

Dylan made sure the exit door was closed securely, and then he caught up with her. Campbell followed more slowly.

Abruptly, the sirens stopped, leaving his ears ringing.

Natasha's long blond hair swung around her shoulders as she settled into a graceful loping stride. Her buttocks and legs were slender, but powerful. Dylan hung back, watching her for a moment before he sped up enough to match her pace.

"Have you talked to Mintz?" she tossed over her shoulder.

"Not yet. The sirens go off whenever any significant weight is put on the fence. Usually they only last a few seconds."

"How'd you know where it was?" She matched her speech pattern to her pace.

Dylan ran alongside her, impressed that she wasn't huffing. She was in damned good shape.

"The sirens have a different repeat for each area."

"Run through them for me."

Dylan recited the litany. "And the front gate is a solid whine. It's the most vulnerable, since it's closest to the main house. I'll have Alfred give you a sheet listing them all."

"That's okay. I've got them. Thanks." She glanced behind her. "Campbell works 24-7?"

Dylan took a quick look back. "He's almost as anxious as I am to get the interface perfected."

"I doubt that."

"He's talented and loyal."

"Yeah? If you say so. Not in very good condition, though." Dylan smiled, hearing Campbell's labored breathing behind them. "Sitting in front of a computer all day will do that."

She sent him a sidelong glance, and then suddenly put out her arm and stopped him. "Hold it."

"What?" They were about fifty feet away from the fence.

"Campbell, stop," she tossed back over her shoulder as she unzipped her fanny pack and drew her weapon.

"Natasha, there's no reason to—"

She gestured with her head. "Just wait here."

Dylan blew out an exasperated sigh. He saw Alfred on the other side of the fence, talking with two of his security guards and two men he didn't recognize.

"What's going on?" Campbell huffed.

"She said to wait."

Natasha approached the fence on the balls of her feet, her weapon ready. Dylan couldn't take his eyes off her. She was graceful, strong and confident. Her pale hair shone like the moon in the darkness of predawn.

"Damn, she is *so* hot," Campbell whispered. "Who'd have thought an FBI agent could look like that?"

Who indeed? Dylan nodded to himself. *Hot* wasn't the word he'd use. *Cool* was more like it. Cool and beautiful, but with a deep undercurrent he couldn't identify. A steel core lurked behind that beautiful skin. A barrier or a firewall? he wondered.

Still, he couldn't deny the heat that surged through him as he watched her run. His reaction to her surprised him. He hadn't felt anything close to a sexual urge in a long, long time.

She turned and gestured for them to come forward.

Dylan stalked up beside her and bent his head near her ear. Her hair teased his nose. "This isn't the first time we've had a breach, you know."

She stiffened and her chin went up a fraction. "Of course not. I apologize, sir."

"Don't. You were only doing your job."

"Not according to your chief of security. He thinks I should stick to the computers."

"Alfred is very territorial."

"That would be an understatement—sir."

Dylan smiled. He took in her profile—her small determined chin, her willowy neck, the slight upward tilt of her nose.

"Dylan."

It was Alfred. Dylan stepped up to the fence. "What happened? Did you catch him?"

With a brisk nod Alfred passed a business card through the wire.

Dylan read the information on the card with disgust, then stuck it in his pocket. "A reporter, naturally. Get him out of here."

Alfred motioned to the two official-looking strangers. "These are the two FBI agents assigned to help us with physical security." Alfred's voice was carefully bland. He wasn't happy about the *help*.

Dylan turned to Natasha. "You know these guys?"

She nodded stiffly. "One of them."

"Introduce me."

She stepped forward just as the men approached.

The dark-haired man walked up to the fence. "Ray Storm." He touched the brim of his baseball cap.

"Special Agent Storm," Dylan said. "Thanks for being here." Storm had the chiseled features and distinct coloring of a Native American.

The second man stepped up. He was taller and bulkier than Storm with the kind of pretty-boy face that had probably gotten him in a lot of trouble in high school.

"This is Special Agent Daniel Gambrini," Storm said.

"Dr. Stryker," Gambrini acknowledged him.

Dylan nodded. "Thanks."

Storm stepped to one side and motioned to Natasha.

Dylan watched them while Alfred described the damage to the fence. Thank God it was minimal.

"Hey, Nat, you doing okay?" Storm said.

Natasha nodded and said something Dylan didn't catch. Then Storm motioned Gambrini over and introduced him to Natasha.

As the agents headed back toward Alfred, Dylan turned his back on the fence. "Another damned reporter," he said to Campbell, who had hung back out of the way. "Get back to the house. You need to get some sleep."

Campbell nodded eagerly and headed toward the house.

"Natasha, you can grab another couple of hours, too."

She didn't move or comment.

He walked past her. "You want to walk with me?"

She glanced at Alfred, who'd just been handed a camera by one of the security guards, then at her fellow agents. She still held her Glock in both hands and stood perfectly balanced, ready for anything. She obviously took every aspect of her job very seriously.

Dylan realized that made her extremely attractive to him.

Dawn was breaking, and the world had turned that colorless gray that made it hard to distinguish light from shadow. Yet her hair still blazed pale gold.

"You didn't know the second agent?"

She shook her head. "He just transferred in. Took the place of an agent who recently resigned to work in a detective agency with his wife."

"But you know Agent Storm?"

She sent him a sidelong glance. "Storm? Best undercover man in the Bureau. You can depend on him." She glanced over her shoulder. "What's going to happen to that reporter?"

"Alfred will threaten him with prosecution and he'll back off. Like I said, this happens occasionally."

She put her weapon away and looked across the lawn toward the house. "A whole lot of money went into designing this place to be totally hidden. How often is occasionally?"

"Every few months or so. It's impossible to remain totally hidden. This time of the year it's worse. Next week is the third anniversary of my wife's death." The words still felt raw in his throat.

"And your son's, as far as the media knows. Right?"

Dylan heard the edge in her voice. She sounded like Alfred. He frowned. "It was the only way I could keep him safe." Not willing to listen to any recriminations, he headed back toward the house. Natasha fell into step beside him.

"Why not let NSA set you up in a secure facility?"

Dylan rounded on her. "What do you know about the NSA's idea of a secure facility?"

"A little, but—"

"They were kind enough to give me a tour of one that's based—well, nearby. Its first level is fifty feet underground."

Natasha's eyes widened.

"My lab would have been on the third level down. The day-care center and the living quarters were on the *fourth* level. NSA offered me two choices. Ben could stay there with me, or he could be placed with strangers under a fake name until I finished their damn project." The idea still sent nausea clawing up from his gut.

"I can't bear to let him out of my sight. He wouldn't understand. He'd think I'd abandoned him." He spoke through clenched teeth. "And I couldn't bury him under fifty feet of rock and dirt, either."

"No—of course not." Her voice sounded strangled. "So you offered them a third choice." She cut her eyes at him then back to the ground in front of them.

What was the matter with her? Dylan's defenses rose immediately. Did she disapprove of his choice? Ben was his son—and he was protecting him in the best way he knew how. "That's right. If they wanted their precious supersoldier, they'd give me what I wanted."

"So they set up this fortress for you, and now you believe Ben is safe." She pressed her lips together in a thin line and wrapped her arms around her middle.

Dylan stared at her. Whatever was hidden under her cool exterior, it was exposed now. She looked haunted. He could understand her being upset about Ben being confined to this place. He hated it, too. But her reaction was out of proportion.

"We wouldn't be here if I didn't think it was safe. Protecting my child is my first priority."

She didn't look at him. Instead she turned her

head and looked at the house. An almost unnoticeable shudder rippled through her.

"Ben is happy here," he said defensively. "He has the run of the entire house. He has his own camouflaged, secure play area with a wading pool and sandboxes and specially built toys."

He wasn't sure why he felt he had to justify himself to her. He just knew that when she looked at him, her green eyes dug deep inside him to a place he hadn't explored in a long time. A place that hurt.

She nodded jerkily.

"Look, *Agent Rudolph*. I love my son. I'm protecting him. Did you see how quickly and easily that intruder was caught? I've got the best security money can buy."

She turned those green eyes on him. "Then why are you still worried about his safety?"

He felt as though she'd head-butted him.

Anger flared in his chest, and a worm of guilt gnawed at his gut. He jammed his hands into his back pockets to keep from clenching his fists. Careful to speak calmly, he gave her the truth.

"Because despite all this, I know there can never be a place safe enough. There is evil in the world, murderers and fanatics who will do anything, even harm an innocent child, to get what they want."

She stopped him with a hand on his arm. "Then explain something to me. If you're so concerned about Ben's safety, why don't you just stop? Tell the NSA to shove their neural interface."

Shock cut through him like lightning. "You think I'm doing this for *them?* For the government?" A harsh laugh scratched his throat. His chest tightened as he tried to wipe away the vision that never left his mind. The sight of that hulking twisted metal at the bottom of the ravine. The sick certainty that it was his fault.

As Natasha watched Dylan's face in the soft light of dawn, the truth hit her like a bucket of icy water.

Ben's awkward braces. His nerve damage. The fervor that burned in his father's eyes.

She'd been so preoccupied with overcoming her own fears and her concern for the child that she'd missed the obvious.

"Oh, my God," she whispered. "The interface. You're doing it for Ben."

Dylan's face registered sadness and desperation. "He's in a growth spurt right now." His voice was tortured. "His body is sucking energy into growing bone. Even with intense physical therapy, the neurological damage is progressing faster than his body can fight it. He's losing muscle, and with loss of muscle goes the loss of nerve tissue." He scrubbed a hand across his face, and started walking again.

"We're so close to success. Campbell is working on the final debugging. He's already finished the prototype implant. It's ninety-nine percent done. But in order for it to work it needs viable nerve and muscle to stimulate. I only have a few weeks before the damage to Ben's body is too great."

"A few weeks?"

He nodded. "I need to implant the interface and tie the microfibers into Ben's nervous system before the nerves that control his legs all die."

Natasha matched her pace to his. "So it's Ben who's running out of time," she said, sadness gripping her heart in its heavy fist.

He nodded. "There aren't enough hours in a day. I could complete it tomorrow, or it could take a year. I've got to believe it will happen tomorrow. If I could, I'd let NSA move the prototype, but it's much too fragile."

"Who'll be operating on Ben?"

Dylan's brows raised. "Me, of course."

She was surprised. "You? Don't you think you're too emotionally involved?"

"It doesn't matter if I am or not. There are only three neurosurgeons in the world who have the expertise to handle this intricate microscopic surgery."

"Only three?"

He nodded grimly. "Two besides me."

"Who are they?"

"There's no way you'd know them. One is Mohan Patel, at the University of Mumbai in India. The other is Frederick Werner. He's at Johns Hopkins. I studied under him."

"Why couldn't one of them do the operation?"

"Because Ben is *my* son." His expression darkened. "I don't need someone else to do the surgery. I've been preparing for this for three years. Besides, it's all moot if I can't complete the nerve mapping in time."

"And the code? It's still buggy?"

"There's at least one more error we can't find." He sighed. "Campbell and I have looked at it too long. We need a fresh eye. And now we've got a hacker trying to steal the code almost certainly to sell to some foreign government. That's why I asked NSA to send me the best."

They reached the entrance to the back stairs. Dylan pressed his thumb against the pad and keyed in the current pass code. He held the heavy security door open for her.

As she walked past him, he caught her arm. His hot touch branded her through the sleeve of her sweater. She looked up and met his haunted gaze.

"Help me debug the computer program. Build a firewall no hacker can get past. Give me the time

I need to finish. If anything happens to the program or the prototype, my son will lose his last chance." His voice cracked. "Do you understand what that means?"

She nodded, thinking of the wire braces propped beside Ben's little bed.

"I doubt you do. In another few weeks, Ben won't even be able to use the braces." Dylan's voice cracked.

Shock and denial pierced her chest. "What do you mean? He seems to handle the braces just fine."

"Once the nerve damage progresses by another ten percent, he won't be able to move his legs at all. The braces will be useless, and my son will be confined to a wheelchair for the rest of his life."

Her heart squeezed painfully. "But I thought the interface—"

His anguished gaze answered her. *Must have viable muscle and nerve.* Not even Stryker's genius could stop the damage from becoming permanent.

She had a fleeting vision of that vital, healthy little boy stuck in a wheelchair, the cold metal sucking the life out of him. Trapped as surely as if he were buried alive.

Nausea swirled through her and a trickle of sweat slid down the back of her neck.

Dylan gripped her arm. "Can you do it?" His

eyes glittered in the dim night. "Can you hold the hacker at bay until I finish the prototype? It's Ben's only chance to be normal."

Chapter Three

The next morning at breakfast, Charlene grudgingly asked Natasha if she'd like to walk outside with her and Ben. "He's had a rough morning already, so we're skipping the morning therapy session."

Charlene's demeanor hardly fit her friendly words. Natasha figured Mintz had ordered her to show Natasha Ben's playground. But the computer equipment wouldn't arrive until around noon, and she wasn't about to give up the chance to see what passed for *outside,* or to find out more about Charlene. "I'd love to."

Natasha changed into a sleeveless white top and jeans, and wove her hair into a French braid. She started to leave her weapon in her room, but changed her mind. She was on duty. She buckled on the fanny pack and stored the Glock inside it.

When she met Ben and Charlene in the atrium, Ben was whiny.

"You said he'd had a rough morning?"

Charlene leaned close to Natasha. "Dr. Stryker examined him. That's always painful for Ben."

"Painful?" Natasha frowned.

Charlene nodded as she took Ben's hand. "Come on, cowboy, let's go outside."

Outside consisted of a play area off the kitchen, about the size of a tennis court, and covered by the camouflage mesh canopy Mintz had told her about. The area was bordered on the back and west by the house, and on the other two sides by a thick evergreen hedge.

"Ben can't go beyond the hedge. Dr. Stryker doesn't take even the smallest chance that someone might get a glimpse of him." Charlene leaned closer. "You know the world thinks Ben died in the accident."

Natasha nodded as she surveyed the play area. Stone paths led through a maze of flowers and shrubs. A little swing set and toys occupied one side of the yard. In the center sat a goldfish pond with a clear acrylic barrier around it, so Ben could see the fish but couldn't fall in.

She looked skyward, then out past the thick hedge. The canopy shaded the manicured play area, while the field beyond the hedge was overgrown and wild, just the kind of place a child would love to run and explore. The kind of place that would put color in Ben's cheeks and make him smile.

"I guess this area gives him some sunlight," she conceded, spreading her hand. The canopy broke the sunlight into dots of light and shadow across her palm.

"He loves it out here, don't you, cowboy?"

But Ben stood beside Charlene, looking dejected.

Charlene held out a soft fuzzy toy helicopter. "Go play."

"I wanna see a real copter," Ben whined.

"There's no real copter today." Charlene sounded bored and irritated. "Play with your toy."

Catching Natasha's eye, she shrugged. "One of the guards showed him a helicopter flying over the field out there one day. Now he's obsessed."

"I want my daddy. Where's Daddy?"

Charlene sighed and put her hand on Ben's shoulder. "Why don't you find a butterfly?" She pointed. "Is that one?"

"Butterfly?" Ben's attention was caught. "Butterfly!" he shouted, moving toward a bed of flowers.

"I really wish Dr. Stryker would examine him in the evening instead of the morning. He's pouty all day afterward."

Natasha dragged her gaze away from Ben's search for the butterfly. "What does an examination entail?"

Charlene outlined the arduous testing, stretching and measuring. Just as she started describing needle stimulation of nerves, a security guard appeared from the house. It was Hector Alvarez. Mintz had introduced them the first night.

With a stealthy glance at Natasha, he spoke to Charlene. "I need to check your pass code device," he said. "Some of them are malfunctioning."

"Sure, Hector." She glanced back toward Ben as she dug in her pocket. "Hey, cowboy, come back this way," she called.

Natasha assessed the guard as Charlene handed him her card. Was he going to check *her* device? The guard grinned and leaned close to whisper in Charlene's ear.

Apparently not.

As Natasha smiled wryly at Hector's ruse to steal a moment alone with Charlene, she became aware of a low rumble and realized the sound had been growing for several seconds. She turned just as it intensified into a rhythmic roar.

"Copter!" Ben squealed in delight.

He was farther away than she'd realized, almost to the hedge.

"Ben, no!" she cried as a helicopter came into view beyond the trees.

From the corner of her eye she saw Charlene

whip around. "Ben, get back here," Charlene shouted.

He disappeared into the tangle of shrubbery.

"Ben!" Natasha ran. She lunged through the hedge, her arms up to protect her face. Limbs and twigs caught at her clothes and hair as she pushed forward against the thick mesh of branches.

She emerged into full sunlight just as the helicopter flew overhead. Ben ran toward its shadow, his braces catching the sun, his arms stretched skyward.

"Copter! Copter!"

Natasha threw herself toward the child.

The helicopter swooped alarmingly low just as she wrapped Ben in her arms and rolled over on top of him. She caught a metallic flash as the downwash from the rotors blew dust and dirt into her eyes.

Metal! Camera or gun?

Instinctively she shielded Ben's body with hers. Her back muscles contracted with the expectation of a bullet.

She heard the *rat-tat-tat* of an automatic weapon. She cringed and tried to spread herself more completely over the shuddering, crying child beneath her.

"It's okay," she whispered, tucking his face into her shoulder. "Close your eyes, sweetie. You're safe."

Dust and grass cuttings swirled around them, stinging her arms and neck as the helicopter rose and sped away.

Somebody put a hand on her shoulder.

"Are you all right?" It was Hector, the guard.

As Natasha sat up, Charlene appeared, her wide, terrified gaze scanning the child's body for injuries.

"Ben! What were you doing? Oh, you bad boy!" She sounded close to hysteria.

She reached for Ben, but he turned to Natasha. Her heart twisted in fear and relief as she gathered him into her arms.

Charlene stopped short.

Ben wailed and clung to Natasha's neck.

"It's okay, sweetie," she whispered, hugging his small body tightly. "I know how scary it is." She rubbed his back and whispered. "I know. I know."

"Give him to me," Charlene said.

But Natasha ignored her and rose without letting go of Ben. She blinked dust out of her eyes. Every inch of her stung where the sharp branches had scratched her.

She surveyed the sky and the surrounding area, but saw nothing. Then she glared at the obviously shaken guard.

He clutched his weapon with white-knuckled

fingers. Faint horror darkened his gaze as he looked her and Ben over. "Is Ben okay, ma'am? Are you?"

"Yes. We're fine. It's Hector, right? Who fired weapons?"

The guard's face was ashen. "Ma'am, I did."

Natasha cradled the back of Ben's head. He buried his nose in her neck. "Was the copter armed? Did you hit it? What did you see?"

The guard stammered. "I—I tried to aim for the landing gear. I don't think I hit anything."

"There was someone leaning out the door. They had either a camera or a gun. You didn't see that?"

He shook his head. "All I saw was a flash of light. My instructions are to defend."

"Not to observe?" Natasha snapped.

"Of course, ma'am." He flushed, red creeping up his neck to his cheeks and ears. "I did the best I could."

Natasha sniffed. "Once you dragged your attention away from Charlene," she muttered.

Hector's eyes narrowed and she caught a flash of anger in them.

She squinted and surveyed the tree line again. "If it was a camera, we'll know soon enough. There will be at least one story about Dr. Stryker's son on the news tonight." She shot a disgusted glance at the guard. "Not to mention the story of ground fire."

She turned her attention back to Ben, wiping his dusty, tear-streaked face with her fingers. He kept his head pressed against her collarbone, his tiny fists clutching her shirt.

She tasted dust and grit. Her face burned where the bushes had scratched it. She examined Ben's arms and face. A few shiny spheres of blood dotted his arms.

"Natasha," Charlene said. "Give Ben to me. I need to take him inside and examine him."

"I've got him." Natasha spoke over Ben's head, struggling to keep her voice steady and soothing. Ben had quit shivering and his crying had changed to quiet sobs. She was not about to let him be upset any further. And right this minute she didn't trust Charlene or Hector as far as she could throw them.

She scanned the hedge and spotted the gate near the boundary. So that's how the two of them had gotten through without a scratch. They'd taken the time to run to the gate.

Sniffing derisively, she shifted Ben's weight to her other side as she headed toward the house. She wasn't about to let him go until she placed him in his father's arms.

"I want Daddy," Ben whined, wriggling.

"I know, sweetie." Natasha pressed a kiss to his damp, grimy cheek.

Mintz appeared at the kitchen door, his face nearly purple with rage.

Natasha stopped in front of him. "Sir, I'm sorry—"

The security chief ruffled Ben's hair and nodded at Natasha. "Good job," he muttered, then he stalked toward the guard.

"Hector, what the hell happened out here?"

Natasha hardly spared a thought for the fate of the inexperienced security guard. She needed to find Dylan.

Ignoring Charlene's voice, and surprised at how natural it suddenly felt to hold and comfort Ben, she stalked through the atrium and into the living quarters.

Dylan met them at the door to Ben's room.

"Daddy!" Ben cried. He twisted and lunged toward his father.

Natasha breathed a sigh of relief as Dylan gathered his son in his strong safe arms.

Dylan fiercely hugged the small, sturdy body that was more precious to him than his own breath.

For a moment he couldn't speak. He just held on to his son as big sobs racked Ben's body. The smell of grass and dirt swirled through his senses.

"Hey, sport, you okay?" Dylan whispered, a catch in his voice. He brushed twigs and dust from his son's hair and inspected the scratches on his face and arms.

"Daddy! I saw a copter! It got close! The wind blew all around! I was scared, Daddy! *Real* scared!"

"I know, sport, I know." He pulled Ben close and kissed his dusty forehead just as Charlene rushed in, her face pallid and streaked with tears.

He glared at her.

"Dr. Stryker, I don't know how it happened. Natasha wanted to go out to the play area with us, and then Hector insisted on seeing my entry card—"

"Stop blubbering," Dylan whispered hotly as he patted his son's back.

He looked at Natasha. Her appearance shocked him. Although her face was composed, she was a mess. Her face was scraped in several places. Her long lashes were white with dust, as were her jeans. Blood dotted her arms and hands where the sharp branches of the hedge had scratched her. An angry gash marred her left arm. Her blond braid was coming undone, and twigs and grass clung to her hair.

He had no doubt what had happened. Of the three people who had been with Ben when the helicopter had flown over, only Natasha had put herself between his child and possible danger. He needed to tighten security around Ben's play area. Now that Agents Storm and Gambrini were helping guard the main gate, Mintz could put an extra guard back there.

"Are you all right?" he asked her gravely.

She nodded.

He glanced over at Charlene. "You. See Alfred."

Charlene looked terrified.

Good. She shouldn't have let Ben get three feet away from her. Alfred would make sure she understood.

"Sir, please. I am *so*—"

"I'm pleased with your skills," he interrupted her. "And Ben likes you. But if anything like this ever happens again—" He couldn't go on. His son clung to him with all his might. His little body still shivered, and his hot tears seared Dylan's neck.

Charlene looked stricken. She'd been Ben's physical therapist since soon after the car crash, and she obviously adored him. But right now Dylan didn't care about her feelings. He didn't care about anything except his son. He wanted to comfort him, make him feel safe.

"Just see Alfred," he said tightly. He waited until Charlene left. Then he turned his attention to Natasha.

Her eyes were riveted on Ben. Their irises were a deep jade-green, surrounded by those long dust-covered lashes.

"Are you sure you're okay?" he asked her.

She looked at him, her eyes wide and worried. "I'm fine. What about Ben—?"

Dylan caressed his son's head. "He'll be fine. Go on," he said gently. "And, thanks."

She started to say something, but stopped herself. She lowered her gaze and went through the connecting door to her room.

He set Ben on his knee and ran his thumb gently across his flushed cheeks, then kissed his dusty forehead, his chest squeezing with fear and relief and love.

Dear God, how would he live if he lost his baby?

"Dad-dy," Ben sniffed.

He hugged his little boy. "I know, sport. I know. Tell Daddy all about the copter."

NATASHA STOOD UNDER the shower, wincing as hot water stung the fresh scrapes and scratches.

The roar of the helicopter still rang in her ears, as did Ben's terrified sobs. His little body had seemed so small and fragile under hers.

The incident had spooked her. At best the helicopter was a news bird, trying to capitalize on the anniversary of Stryker's wife's death and the rumors about his son. At worst it was one of the fringe groups NSA was concerned about. Groups of radical fanatics interested in stealing and profiting from the neural interface technology.

Dylan was convinced that Ben was safe here. He would never agree to go to a secure facility, or send his son away. After hearing his horror story about the NSA's underground "safe house," Natasha couldn't blame him.

But part of her was afraid that Mintz was right. As much as it horrified her to think about it, her rational mind knew that Ben and Dylan would be safer behind fortified, guarded walls. This compound, as protected as it was, was still vulnerable.

She knew Dylan believed he could protect his son. Now that she knew him, she believed it, too. Seeing his fierce determination, his intense devotion to Ben, she was almost convinced that he *could* single-handedly protect him from the world. It was obvious that Ben would be devastated if he were taken away from his father.

Whatever Dylan wanted, she'd make it happen. She just needed to be more careful, more aware, more vigilant.

She raised her head to the shower spray,

wishing the water could wash away her fear and guilt.

She knew she wasn't without blame. She should have stayed close enough to Ben to prevent him from getting near the hedge. Even the warm glow of appreciation she'd seen in Dylan's eyes hadn't made her feel better.

Because she knew the truth. There had been a moment out there—a brief moment when she had thought about taking Ben's hand and leading him through the hedge into the unfettered light of the sun.

To her horror, she realized she could just as easily have exposed Ben to danger as shielded him.

Eager to wash away the surge of regret, she turned the hot water up higher and scrubbed at her wounds, grimacing as the soap stung them.

DYLAN DRIFTED AWAKE with a surprising sense of safety and calm. He opened his eyes and saw his son's beautiful face. Ben was asleep, his little mouth moving with soft breaths. There were traces of tears on his cheeks.

Dylan's heart swelled until his chest could hardly hold it. He loved Ben so much his whole body ached with it.

On the day he'd been told his infant son would

never walk, he'd dedicated his life to proving the doctors wrong.

He'd worked for NSA since before Ben was born. NSA wanted bionic capabilities. Dylan had agreed to expand his research and develop the technology. It had turned out to be a fatal decision. It had cost him his wife and nearly his son.

So he'd demanded impossible concessions, half hoping they'd leave him alone. But the government had met every demand. They'd even agreed to help him hide Ben's existence from the world. They wanted their supersoldier that badly.

All Dylan wanted was to give his son the ability to walk. The NSA's offer provided unlimited funding, so he'd agreed. He'd built a fortress to shield Ben, and gone to work on the neural interface.

But now, his worst fear was realized. He and all he held dear were under attack again. A hacker had tried to penetrate his computer files, and within two days there were two efforts to breach the security of his estate. Were they connected?

Ben stirred, as if sensing his father's agitation. With a sigh, Dylan checked his watch. He'd dozed for about twenty minutes. He kissed the top of Ben's head, then a little scratch above his eyebrow.

He needed to get back down to the lab. He was nearly done mapping the nerves. If Natasha could hold off the hacker long enough, Campbell could finish debugging the program, and Dylan could test it one last time. Then they could encase it in the specially built box, and NSA could transport it, along with Dylan and Ben, to whatever secret government location they wished.

Once he was satisfied that Ben's surgery was successful, Dylan planned to wash his hands of the damned interface, the government and the encroaching danger. Maybe once it was out of his hands, he could be sure his child was truly safe.

Moving quietly, he got up and glanced at the connecting door that led to *his* room, the room he'd vacated when Natasha had arrived. He was spending most of his time in the lab, and he liked the idea that Charlene was on one side of Ben and Natasha was on the other.

Natasha had looked ill by the time she'd gone into her room. Had she just been feeling the reaction to the close call with the helicopter, or had she been hurt worse than he'd realized?

The sight of her grimy, scratched face, eyes dark with concern for Ben, rose in his mind. He'd already seen how seriously she took her job, but today, she'd earned his admiration and trust, and his undying gratitude. She'd protected his child without thought to her own safety.

He needed to check on her. To thank her. After

slipping on his shoes, he tiptoed over to the door and knocked lightly.

No answer. He wasn't surprised. Natasha didn't seem like the type to waste time or indulge herself when there was work to be done. She'd probably already cleaned up and gone down to the lab. He knocked again.

Behind him, Ben stirred. Not wanting to wake him, Dylan turned the knob and slipped through the door.

"Natasha?" he called.

No sign of her, except her dusty clothes tossed in a corner. Oh well, he'd catch up with her in the lab. As he started toward the hall door, he heard a faint noise behind him.

The bathroom door opened and she emerged, one hand toweling her wet hair, the other pulling a very short, very damp purple satin robe closed.

"Oh." Her eyes widened.

Her face, her neck, the hollow between her breasts, gleamed with dampness. Every curve of her body was unmistakably outlined by the wet satin. Her concave belly and delicate navel were exposed to Dylan's hungry view, as was the golden glistening shadow between her legs.

To his surprise, his body reacted immediately and urgently. Suddenly, he grew hard, his arousal throbbing with a delicious ache against the constricting seam of his jeans. Desire, hot and unfamiliar, streaked through him.

Twice in less than twenty-four hours he'd reacted sexually to Natasha Rudolph.

Twice. Yet he couldn't remember the last time he'd been attracted to a woman. The last time he'd felt anything at all other than the fear that he wouldn't be able to save Ben's legs.

She yanked her robe closed, and let the towel drop to the floor. His jaw ached as the terry cloth slid down her legs—legs that went on forever, smooth and creamy. He raised his gaze, tracing the strong shapely thighs back up until they disappeared under the very short robe.

His gaze continued upward. Her breasts had tightened. The thin wet fabric revealed each puckered ridge of her nipples.

His mouth went dry as he imagined the taste of them. "I'm sorry—" he croaked.

"Did you—" she said at the same time. "Did you need something? Is Ben okay?"

His gaze flew to her face. "Your face is bleeding," he whispered hoarsely.

Her eyes, starred by her pale wet lashes, widened. She shook her head. "Just scratches," she said tightly, releasing one edge of her robe to touch a scrape on her cheek.

He moaned deep in his throat.

She blinked. She'd heard him.

Get it together, he admonished himself as she clutched the robe together more tightly.

She moistened her lips. It was a nervous gesture, since her face and mouth were still damp from the shower. The sight of her tongue nearly sent him over the edge.

He had to get out of there before he embarrassed himself. He clenched his jaw and took a step backward, as if being a foot farther away from her would break the spell of desire she'd cast over him.

"I wanted to thank you…" Breathless, he stopped, rubbing the back of his neck. "Look. I'll leave so you can dress."

She shook her head. "You don't have to thank me. I did what anyone would do."

"No. Two of my trusted employees were there, and yet the only person who protected Ben without thought to her own safety was you."

"I scared him." Regret pooled in her eyes like tears. "I didn't mean to—"

A thin drop of blood trickled from just above her wrist. Without thinking, he stepped close to her and pushed up the sleeve of her robe. Ugly red scratches covered her arms. He ran a finger along her forearm. "Some of these are bad. We should get them bandaged. There's a first aid kit in the bathroom. In the cabinet."

She looked up at him.

"This is my room," he said with a shrug.

She'd suspected it. Although his clothes were gone, there was a stark masculinity about the room. And of course, he'd sleep next door to Ben.

But he'd put her in his room, and now she was sleeping in his bed, using his shower, standing naked in the same room where he'd stood naked. The vision that accompanied her thoughts was vivid, erotic…and impossible. She bit the inside of her cheek to stop the delicious, dangerous daydreams.

"Let me help you with those scratches—" He stepped closer.

"I can take care of them," she murmured.

"I can't tell you how grateful I am."

A drop of water fell from her lashes to her cheek, and a spear of longing pierced him.

"Your son is very special," she said.

He nodded.

She lifted her head a fraction of an inch, her pale lashes making her eyes seem wider and greener. He traced his thumb across her wrist.

She stiffened and pulled her hand away.

Suddenly jarred out of the mesmerizing haze of desire, he was embarrassed at how natural and necessary it had seemed that he touch her.

He backed away. "Okay then. I'll leave you to

dress." He turned on his heel. At the hall door he stopped. "By the way, your equipment is here."

"I'll get right to work. I was on my way to the lab."

Dylan disappeared through the door.

Natasha's hand flew to her mouth. She sucked in a long, shaky breath as she looked down at herself. A sharp, thrilling shiver tightened her thighs. She'd been practically naked, with Dylan Stryker's blazing eyes on her—on every part of her.

She wiped her face with both hands.

Concentrate, she admonished herself. She didn't have time for an adolescent crush on the handsome doctor. She had to get her new equipment installed and catch a hacker.

FOURTEEN HOURS LATER Tom's fist squeezed the phone. He'd listened to enough babbling. He was sick of it. "Shut up! I just want to know one thing. Are you ready?"

"Yes, but—"

"Good, because it's going down right now. Are you sure the west door is unlocked?"

"I checked it myself, an hour or so ago. I almost got caught. I heard somebody on the back stairs."

"At three o'clock in the morning? Who?"

"I didn't see them."

"And they didn't see or hear you, right?"

"Of course not."

"You'd better hope not. Call me as soon as you can. Remember, we're not expecting this to cause any real damage. We just want to convince Stryker that his kid's not safe there. That news helicopter fiasco should make it even easier."

He hadn't missed the significance of the video he'd seen earlier on the local news. The woman who had thrown herself over the child to protect him was *his* Natasha. He had no doubt. He knew that pale hair, the long shapely body, the efficiency of movement. She hadn't changed, except that she looked stronger, more substantial, than she had eight years ago when she was a teenage runaway looking for a job.

"Did you see the news?" his caller asked. "That was her—"

"I told you to shut up. Concentrate on your job. And let me know everything that happens."

"I'll do my best."

"No. You'll *do* exactly as I tell you! What the hell do you think I have you in there for?"

He tossed his cell phone down onto the bed and paced. The truck was on its way, its fanatical driver prepared to ram it into Dylan Stryker's front gate going a hundred miles an hour.

That was one point in favor of working with a bunch of zealots who were willing, even eager, to die for their cause. They were so malleable—they actually longed for a leader, someone who could convince them to sacrifice their lives for their beliefs.

And *he* was the man for the job. He shook his head in wry disbelief. There was nothing he could think of that was worth dying for.

Killing, however. That was another matter entirely. He wouldn't hesitate to kill to obtain Dr. Stryker's interface.

He'd worked patiently to gain back the headway he'd lost three years ago with the botched kidnapping of Stryker's wife. He'd lurked in Stryker's computer for months, reading every e-mail, watching Stryker's buying habits. His suspicion was true. Stryker's son had survived. And Stryker was working harder than ever to perfect his technique for the surgical implant of the interface.

So he'd put his plan into motion, recruiting people, studying Stryker, patiently waiting for an opportunity to infiltrate his defenses.

Now the government had unwittingly sent in his nemesis to stop him. It couldn't have been more perfect. Although Natasha presented a challenge, she hadn't been as good as he was back then, and she wasn't now.

Still, he was glad he'd had the foresight to put

together a backup plan. Backups were essential. Any good hacker knew that. His plan depended on leverage, and he'd soon have access to the best leverage of all—Stryker's son.

He couldn't get to the boy inside the estate. Penetrating that fortress would mean taking an unnecessary risk. He had to wait until Stryker decided to move the kid. He was surprised the neurosurgeon hadn't already done that. Obviously, Stryker needed more motivation.

Tom stretched out on his unmade bed. With the help of his contact on the inside, he'd supply that motivation.

Stryker would soon be exactly where he wanted him. The surgeon had always been weak when it came to family. He'd give up the interface in a heartbeat to save his little boy.

Then he could sell it to the highest bidder. Hell, to all the bidders. It *was* freeware. He chuckled at his joke. Even if it was encrypted, it was no problem. He could break the encryption in no time.

After all, he was still the best.

NATASHA COULDN'T SLEEP. She'd finished installing the new equipment on her computer. Then she'd searched Dylan's encrypted program files. To her relief, she'd found no trace of the hacker there.

By ten o'clock, she'd been nodding and yawning, so she'd set a simple but effective 128-bit encryption that would work with the existing security to protect the system until morning, then dragged herself upstairs to bed.

Mintz had let her know that there was a news story on a couple of the local channels—renewing speculation about Dylan's son. They had video, Mintz told her, showing two figures.

She turned over and squeezed her eyes shut, trying to find a cool place on the pillow, but the sheets scraped her raw arm, reminding her of the gentleness of Dylan's touch.

She'd felt stripped bare in front of him. Her body had thrummed with awareness as she endured his smoky gaze. There was no denying that he was devilishly handsome and sexy, but that wasn't all that drew her to him.

It was his fire, his brooding passion. The focused intensity with which he approached everything from his research to his protective care of his son.

He loved Ben. But Mintz was right. Love was not enough. Her parents had loved her. But they'd died.

She didn't want to be a part of separating Ben from his father. She hated that Mintz was right. But he was, and she had to help him convince Dylan that Ben would not be safe until he let him go.

A deep rumble shook her bed.

Oh, God! Her eyes flew open. *An explosion?* Her heart leaped into her throat and blinding fear threatened to paralyze her.

The sirens were close. Too close. And no repeat. She remembered Dylan's list of signals.

Someone had breached the front gate.

Chapter Four

The siren's screech distorted in Natasha's ears as she groped under her pillow for her weapon. Her heart pounded frantically in her chest and shock reverberated through her.

The front gate. A direct attack.

She thrust her feet into her boots and pulled on a sweater. She buckled on her fanny pack and crossed the room, flattening her back against the wall next to the door.

When she eased the door open, the siren's screech intensified, hurting her ears. She darted a quick look into the hall, but saw no one, so she angled around the door, leading with her gun.

A noise to her right made her whirl, her weapon trained. It was Charlene's door. The girl's pale face and wide eyes shone in the dim hall light. She eyed Natasha's gun with undisguised terror.

Natasha sidled toward her, glancing behind her

every few seconds. "What's happened? Do you know?" she asked.

Charlene clawed at her neck above the dainty blue nightgown. "Something triggered the alarm at the gate." She sent a worried look toward the atrium. "But I've never heard sirens go on this long."

"I'm going to check it out. Get back inside," she commanded, putting her mouth close to Charlene's ear. "Ben's going to be scared."

"Don't you think I know that?" she yelled. "Ben is my charge and Dr. Stryker is my boss. You're trying to get into his good graces by undermining me. Well it won't work. He's—"

"Get Ben's braces on him," Natasha snapped.

Charlene blinked.

"If we need to move him, I want him ready."

Charlene bristled. Natasha held her gaze. Finally Charlene nodded and stepped inside her room and closed the door.

Natasha moved quickly toward the atrium. As she approached the doorway, a different blare filled her ears and the door in front of her swung shut. She lunged for it as the latch clicked into place.

"No!" Her heart jumped into her throat as she wrenched the doorknob. Mintz had told her about the lockdown sequence, designed to protect the living quarters in case of a breach of the estate's walls.

Panic constricted her throat. She was trapped. She struggled to breathe. She had to get out—now!

Frantically, berating herself for her weakness, she rattled the knob, then stared down at it.

Think! The fingerprint pad was right beside the knob. Where was her pass code device? She unzipped her fanny pack and dug inside.

A hand touched her bare shoulder. A hot strong hand. She tensed. Her right hand tightened around her weapon even as her senses told her whose hand it was.

Dylan.

"I've got it." He pressed his thumb onto the pad and then keyed in the pass code. The lock clicked.

Her breath whooshed out in relief as she pushed the door open.

He squeezed her shoulder. "Ben's in his room?"

"I told Charlene to put his braces on and wait."

Dylan sent her an approving glance. "Good. She's been with him most of his life. He feels safe with her."

They slipped through the door and Dylan pushed it closed. The atrium was empty, but Natasha saw men in dark clothing moving about outside.

"What's going on?" she whispered.

He shook his head and rubbed his stubbled cheek. "I can't reach Alfred. After the excitement this afternoon and the news story tonight, it's probably another reporter trying to force his way past the guardhouses. I don't know what the explosion was. Usually one of the night guards would have turned off the sirens by now."

She wished the guard would hurry up. The noise was grating on her nerves and hurting her ears. Her neck and shoulders ached with tension, and her head was beginning to pound.

Clenching her jaw, she pushed through the two sets of glass doors that formed a small foyer just beyond the atrium. Dylan followed right behind her.

Hector was standing with Robby, another guard she'd met when she'd arrived. They held their weapons at the ready, and stared up the long drive toward the front gate.

Robby turned at their approach. "Dr. Stryker, someone hit the gate. You can see the smoke above the trees. Mintz told us to stay here and guard the front entry to the house."

"You don't know who's responsible?" Dylan asked.

"No, sir. We haven't heard anything since Mintz went out there."

Natasha jogged several steps up the driveway

until she spotted the obelisk silhouette of the massive gates. Above them, rising up to obscure the stars, was a growing mushroom of thick black smoke.

She broke into a run.

"Natasha!"

Dylan sprinted up beside her and grabbed her arm. She was forced either to slow down or lose her balance.

"Whoa. What are you doing?" His fingers tightened, burning her flesh.

"My job." She panted in rhythm with her steps. She tried to twist out of his grasp. "You should get back inside until we know what happened."

"Me? What about you?"

Irritation flared inside her as she rounded on him. "I'm an FBI agent. You're unarmed."

Dylan's sharp gaze glided over her from head to toe and his mouth turned up. She sent him a disgusted look. She was aware of how she looked, dressed in a black cotton sweater over pink cropped pajama bottoms with lacy hems, wearing hiking boots and a leather fanny pack, and carrying a Glock.

Light flared against the black smoke as something caught fire. Dylan headed toward the gates.

This time Natasha stopped him. "Dylan, wait. Whatever happened out there is aimed at you and your son. Ben is probably terrified and wanting his father—especially after his scare this afternoon." She gestured back toward the house. "Why don't you go be with him? We can take care of this."

He glanced back at the house, running a hand across the back of his neck. His expression reflected his struggle. He wanted to be with his son, but he also wanted to see for himself that his estate was still secure.

She remembered what she'd thought the first time she'd seen him. He was burning himself out. A wave of compassion caught her off guard.

Just then the mobile radio clipped to the waistband of his jeans crackled. He unclipped it and listened.

Natasha only caught a couple of words. *Truck. Explosives.*

"Alfred, open the side gate."

"No." The word cracked like lightning through the radio.

She agreed with Mintz. Dylan was the last person who should be on the other side of that gate right now.

Mintz said something else.

"Then you come in here and tell me what's going on," Dylan snapped. "Now!"

He clipped the radio back on his hip and

muttered a curse. He paced, flexing his right hand, doubling it into a fist, then flexing it again.

"Dylan."

A heated frown was his only response.

"Dylan." She laid a hand on his tense forearm. "You shouldn't pull Mintz away from the scene right now."

He ran a hand over his face. "He's not in charge anymore," he said bitterly.

"He's not? You mean my agents have taken over?"

"They aren't in charge, either. The *scene* has been taken over by the police. Apparently, not only must I have the FBI crawling all over my private property, I can't even keep the damn cops off."

Natasha took a deep breath as she eyed the smoke billowing above the twenty-foot gate. The air was tainted with the odors of gasoline, oil and other less-pleasant odors. Smoke stung her nostrils.

"That's how it's done," she commented. "The entrance to your estate is now a crime scene."

He sent her a glare worthy of a laser scalpel.

She met his glare, shook her head and turned back to the rising smoke. "You really think you can control everything, don't you?"

"*No.* Alfred says the same thing. You're both wrong. I just want to know what's going on."

"The very definition of control freak," she muttered.

"What did you say?"

A noise to their left caught her attention. She stepped around Dylan and raised her weapon just as Mintz appeared through a steel mesh door obscured by a tall hedge, accompanied by a dour-faced man in a rumpled suit.

The stern man eyed Natasha's Glock and swept his suit coat back to reveal his weapon and shield. A police detective.

Natasha lowered her weapon. She dipped into her fanny pack and pulled out her own badge. "Special Agent Rudolph. FBI."

The detective nodded. "Frank Buckram. Homicide."

Dylan's shoulder brushed hers as he stepped forward. "I'm Dylan Stryker. Did you say homicide?"

"Yes, sir," Detective Buckram said.

"What the hell is going on?" Dylan looked at his trusted friend, whose face was creased with worry and smudged with soot. That Alfred was shaken alarmed him. "Are you all right?"

He nodded and squeezed Dylan's shoulder with his big rough hand. The gesture both comforted and worried Dylan. It was Alfred's version of a hug.

"The vehicle was an old delivery truck,"

Buckram continued. "Apparently the driver was on a suicide mission. The truck was a rolling bomb."

The words slammed into Dylan with the impact of .38 slugs. "Bomb? Suicide?" He looked from Alfred to the detective to Natasha.

Her jaw was set, her face fiercely controlled. She exchanged a glance with the detective. Had she been expecting something like this?

Had Alfred? Was that why the ex-POW who'd rather chew rifle slugs than have anyone tell him what to do had been so adamant about accepting the FBI's help?

"I don't get it. Are you saying somebody deliberately blew themselves up trying to get through the gates?"

"Yep. Could be one of those terrorist fringe groups. We'll have to wait and see who claims responsibility." Buckram pulled out a notepad. "You're working on some secret government project, right?"

Dylan grimaced. "You could say that."

Natasha moved closer. "What do you know so far, Detective?" she asked.

Buckram looked up from under his brows. "Not much. My men are still assessing the situation. The truck has no license plate, and we haven't recovered a Vehicle Identification Number. Our CSU will be here in a few minutes."

Alfred spoke. "They've got the surveillance disks from the two guardhouses the truck broke through. Only took him about eleven seconds the way he was driving."

The detective bobbed his head up and down. "Chances are slim to none, but we're hoping to get an ID on the driver or the vehicle."

"Hold it." Dylan wiped his face. "How many people are going to be involved in this? I can't have investigators and police running around all over the place."

"You don't have a choice, son," Alfred said. "It's out of our hands. Until we know otherwise, they're treating this as a homicide, a possible terrorist act."

"Fine. As long as Ben and the lab are safe. Buy me enough time to finish."

He turned to Natasha. "As soon as I can get the implant inserted into Ben's back, attach all the fibers and make sure it's compatible with his immune system and the computer, the FBI and the NSA and whatever other letters want it can have the whole stinking thing. I don't care."

How much more death was there going to be because of him? He'd give his life to make his son whole, but he'd never imagined that his dream of creating a computerized connection between the brain and the body would drive people to murder—or suicide.

"When I developed the capability of stimulating nerves artificially, I envisioned it giving paraplegics the ability to walk, providing nerve-damaged patients with a way to be free of wheelchairs and braces, maybe even some day replacing damaged ears and eyes." He rubbed his face. "I never considered creating supermen who could wage superwars."

He met Natasha's gaze and saw understanding in her green eyes.

Alfred glanced back toward the house. "Ben with Charlene?"

"Yeah," Dylan said. "Natasha told her to get him into his braces, in case we needed to move him."

Natasha's expression changed to alarm. She turned to Buckram. "Detective, what purpose did the bomb at the gate serve?"

Dylan heard the controlled concern in her voice. *What purpose?* He looked at Alfred, who was rubbing his palm over his short-cropped hair. He was worried, too, and that scared Dylan.

"That's what I was wondering," Alfred said. "That truck's not big enough to do any damage to speak of. We'll probably have a couple of marks on the gate and some burned grass, but that's it."

"So what was the point? A demonstration? A publicity stunt for their warped cause?" Natasha's tone sharpened. "Don't these guys usually sacrifice their lives for *something?* Not just for show?"

Her knuckles whitened as she gripped her weapon. "There's something else going on."

A metallic voice from the two-way radios drowned out the end of her sentence. Mintz grabbed his. "Mintz, here."

"This is Robby. You need to see this, sir."

"What is it?"

"A breach, sir. A section of fence on the west side has been cut."

"Did he say breach?" Dylan's pulse hammered and a stinging sensation crawled across his skin.

Alfred stiffened. "Put guards on the fence," he barked. "Get a search organized. Account for everyone."

The gruff words ripped through him. "Oh, God! Ben." His heart froze.

Natasha's face drained of color.

"Ben!" He took off running back to the house. He pumped his arms, reaching for more speed. His damn loafers slipped on the pavement.

He heard the crunch of gravel over his shoulder. Someone was running behind him, catching up. *Natasha.*

By the time he reached the covered drive in front of the front doors, the two-way radio crackled with the sound of Alfred's voice, barking more orders.

A guard spotted them and threw the doors wide. Dylan and Natasha entered shoulder to shoulder. They turned toward the living quarters and burst through the doors.

Dylan skidded to a halt in front of Ben's door and put out a hand to stop Natasha. She bumped into him from behind.

He struggled to pull oxygen into his lungs. If Ben was in there, and unharmed—*please God*— he didn't want to scare him.

Natasha hung back, instinctively understanding his brief pause. He wiped his face. She was waiting for him to make the first move.

He turned the knob and pushed open the door. *Nothing.* The room was empty.

"Ben!" he shouted as his heart shattered. "Ben!"

Natasha pushed past him and swept the room. She nudged open the closet door, then swung her weapon around.

She caught his gaze and nodded toward the door that connected Ben's room with Charlene's.

Dylan acknowledged her, then stepped over to the door. He opened it, standing aside so she had a clear shot if she needed it.

She moved like a cat as she stepped silently through the door, her weapon ready.

Dylan followed, flipping on the lights.

"Empty," Natasha said. Her gaze went to

Charlene's closet. She nodded at Dylan, who eased along the wall toward the door.

The door to Ben's room burst open.

Natasha jerked around, aiming her Glock.

Mintz entered, breathing hard.

"Alfred?"

"I've got men searching the house and the grounds," Alfred said.

Dylan grabbed his arm, partly to draw strength from his friend, but Alfred seemed just as shaken as he was.

"Have you searched the whole wing?" Alfred asked.

Dylan shook his head. "Just in here—"

"Daddy?"

The small muffled voice sheared Dylan's breath.

Natasha whirled instinctively and aimed at the closet door.

Dylan reached for the doorknob but Natasha grabbed his arm. "Wait. Get back."

Alfred stalked past them and with a nod at Natasha, he twisted the knob and opened the closet door. Natasha's arms straightened and her finger tightened on the trigger.

Underneath the hanging clothes were two pairs of feet, one pair locked into braces.

Dylan gasped. He hadn't even realized he'd been holding his breath.

Ben's head stuck out through hanging dresses. His face lit up and he shot out of Charlene's arms. "Daddy!"

Dylan crouched down. As his child flung himself at him, he wrapped his arms around him and lifted him. "Hey, sport." His voice broke and he buried his nose in Ben's bubble-gum scented hair.

Natasha stepped closer to the closet door.

"Come out of there," she said to Charlene crisply, her attention half on Dylan and Ben. Every time she saw them together, her insides twisted into knots, sending a mixture of longing and emptiness through her.

She couldn't watch Dylan hugging his child and not be affected by the sight. Still, she did her best to ignore the imagined feel of those arms comforting and shielding her, or the fantasy of herself as a part of that loving embrace.

Charlene crawled out of the closet and stood, folding her arms around herself. Her face was pale and distorted in terror. "Is everything okay?" she asked.

Natasha nodded, watching her closely. "Why didn't you answer? You must have heard Dr. Stryker calling."

Charlene shook her head. "I couldn't be sure about the voice."

"What do you mean?"

"I had trouble getting Ben's braces on. The sirens terrified him. We sat on his bed, but then I heard something."

"What did you hear?"

"The slamming of a door, or maybe wood cracking. The noise came from the direction of the stairs, so I didn't want to take him through that hall. I brought him in here."

"You're going to need to talk with the detective," Natasha said.

"Detective? Police?" Charlene's eyes showed white all the way around the irises. "What happened? Is everyone all right?"

Natasha nodded, glancing at Dylan.

He shifted Ben to one arm. "Charlene, thank you for taking care of Ben. Tell Alfred everything you heard and saw. I'm going to stay with Ben for a while, until he falls asleep."

As Alfred and Charlene left, Dylan aimed a warning look at Natasha. "Come and get me in an hour. Alfred will do his best to talk you into letting me sleep longer."

An hour later Natasha shrugged tension from her shoulders as she stepped through the hidden gate beside the massive entrance. She was weak with relief that Ben was all right. She'd thought about going back to her room, but she knew there was no way she'd sleep. So she'd come out to see what, if anything, was going on at the scene of the bombing.

Storm looked around as she emerged from the shrubbery.

She had no idea how he always knew when someone was approaching him. He had some sort of sixth sense, a talent inherited from his Native American ancestors she was sure.

"Anything new?" she asked him.

He nodded toward a dark sedan. "Buckram's leaving now. Like he said, there's not much to go on. They're loading what's left of the delivery truck to take back to the lab."

As he spoke, a monstrous dump truck hoisted the charred wet mess in a massive scoop and dropped it into the bed. White and black smoke belched out from the truck bed.

"Think they'll find anything?"

He shrugged. "Who knows? They'll sift through it. But that fire was superhot. Burned everything to a crisp. Whoever made the bombs did that on purpose."

"Terrorists?"

"Buckram figures the driver was probably a foreign national, in the U.S. illegally. If that's true, it's going to take weeks to sort out who he was."

"I guess it won't do any good to try to match dental records or DNA."

"If we're lucky, the guy will be in our terrorist database. But it's a long shot. Even if he is it's going to be a slow process. If they were dumb enough not to file off the Vehicle ID number, or if any papers survived the fire, we might get lucky."

As the truck pulled away, Natasha walked closer to the gates. "Like Mintz said, there's hardly a mark."

"Buckram took a list of Stryker's staff and the surveillance disks from the two guardhouses and from the camera mounted beside the gates."

"Why didn't you take them?"

Storm sent her his million-dollar smile. "'Cause I'm undercover, sugar. I don't have access to the labs and equipment here. It's probably best that no one know that there's more than one FBI agent on the scene."

"Even Buckram?"

Storm nodded just as his gaze sharpened. A couple of seconds later she heard footsteps. She turned in time to see Mintz emerge from the hidden gate.

"You shouldn't be out here," he said, glowering at her. "Get back to the house and catch a couple of hours sleep. Today's going to be busy, and you still have a hacker to catch."

She glanced at Storm, who chuckled.

"Where's Dylan? With Ben?"

She nodded. "Ben was really scared. Dylan lay down with him. He wanted me to wake him in an hour. He said you'd try to keep me from bothering him."

A crack appeared in Mintz's weathered face. Must have been a smile. But then it was gone. "Come on, I'll walk you back."

Natasha raised her brows at the unexpected offer.

"See you later, sugar," Storm said.

"Bye, Storm."

She went through the gate behind Mintz and fell into step beside him.

"Dylan's exhausted," he muttered. "It's a wonder he can think. But he won't stop. Acts like he has a personal vendetta against Ben's disability."

"Burning himself up from the inside."

Mintz shot her a look. "Good way of putting it."

At the front doors, Natasha paused, hands on her hips. "You look like hell yourself, Mr. Mintz. You're covered with soot and mud. Have *you* had any sleep?"

As usual, Mintz didn't answer her question directly. "It's been a long night."

"I vote we let Dylan and Ben sleep, what do you say?"

His sharp brown eyes studied her. "What about you? You didn't get any sleep, either."

Natasha stretched her arms and arched her neck. "I had a couple of hours before the excitement. I think I'll take a shower and then get started tracing that hacker."

DYLAN AWOKE IN A PANIC. *Someone had tried to break in.* His eyes flew open and he saw the small dark head of his son.

Ben was lying on his back with a small fist curled close to his chin. His beautiful little face was placid, his long dark eyelashes resting on his round cheeks, his little mouth moving with his soft breaths.

He was so innocent, so vulnerable. Dylan's heart swelled until he felt his chest couldn't hold it. He loved Ben so much his whole body ached with it. His eyes stung and his throat grew tight.

All he wanted was to make everything right for his child—give him a perfectly functioning body, let him run and play in a world where there were no fences, no confining braces, no people who could hurt him.

But he couldn't rewrite the past or change the present. Someone had deliberately run his wife's car off the road and killed her and maimed his son. The love inside him morphed into helpless fury as the awful memory of the twisted wreckage of the SUV rose in his mind.

And now, despite all his careful efforts, he was under attack again.

Ben stirred, some part of his sleeping brain noticing his father's agitation.

Sighing, Dylan lifted his arm to look at the lighted dial of his watch. Almost seven. *Damn it.* Alfred had talked Natasha into letting him sleep.

He didn't have time to sleep. He needed to get back to work. He was almost done mapping the nerves. As soon as Natasha and Campbell finished debugging the program, he could enclose the delicate prototype in its protective case and turn it over to NSA to be transported to their ultrasecure medical facility.

The only thing he cared about was implanting the computer interface into Ben's spinal cord. The actual operation wouldn't take but about twelve hours. But then they had to wait to see if his little body accepted the foreign object, and if the fibers' computerized stimulation actually worked on human nerves. So many *ifs*.

Once Ben's surgery was successful, Dylan planned to wash his hands of the damned interface, the government and everything and everybody connected with it.

Maybe then, he could feel assured that his child was safe.

He slipped out of bed, doing his best not to disturb Ben. His mobile radio chirruped.

That's what had awoken him, he realized as he unhooked the radio. "Yeah?" he whispered.

"Dylan, are you in Ben's room?"

It was Alfred, and Dylan didn't like his tone. He glanced back at Ben, who was still sleeping peacefully, then slipped through the door to the hall.

"Yeah. What's up?"

"I'll be right there."

Dylan pocketed his phone, frowning. Alfred sounded worried.

The door to Natasha's room opened and she stepped out, dressed in a black sweater and black pants and carrying her work boots. She'd pulled her hair back in a ponytail, and her toes peeked out from under the pants legs.

Dylan dragged his gaze away from her delicate pink toes. "You were supposed to wake me an hour ago. Why didn't you?" he challenged her.

She didn't answer his question. "Mintz just called me. What's up?" She set her boots on the floor and stepped into them, securing the Velcro fasteners.

Dylan shook his head just as Alfred entered through the east door.

"Robby and Hector just notified me that they've finished examining the fence and sweeping the area with infrared detectors, looking for human life. If someone got in, they're gone now." He frowned. "Problem is, Hector found a few fibers caught on a wire—on the inside. They would have been torn away as someone climbed *out*."

"Did Hector get photos before he removed the fibers?" Natasha snapped.

"Robby did."

"Good. Let's get them to the FBI photo-analysis lab. They can let us know if it looks like the fibers were planted."

Dylan watched Alfred. Something more was bothering him. "Alfred, what else? This isn't about just a broken piece of fence."

Alfred shook his head. "Come with me."

"Damn it, Alfred. What is it?"

Alfred didn't speak. He just turned on his heel.

Dylan glanced at Natasha. "Wake Charlene and tell her to watch Ben."

Natasha nodded.

When Dylan got outside, Robby was waiting with Alfred. The three of them started toward the west side of the house. Natasha caught up with them halfway down the hill.

Robby pointed as they approached the secured basement door that led to the back stairway that joined the living quarters to the lab. Reflective orange tape blocked off the area right around the door.

"There are footprints leading up to this door." He glanced at Alfred.

Alfred met Dylan's gaze. "The door is unlocked."

"Unlocked? Are you sure?" Anyone could have gotten to Ben. He rounded on the young guard. "What have you found?"

Robby stepped carefully up to the orange tape and pointed. "They're right here, sir. I've taken pictures, but unfortunately, they appear to be generic rubber garden boots that can be bought anywhere. We'll be lucky if we can estimate the size of the intruder's feet."

"Thank you." Alfred dismissed him.

Dylan stared at Alfred, fear for his son's safety burning a hole in his gut. "What can we do? Shouldn't we be searching? We've got to find this guy before—" He couldn't even form the words.

"Dylan—" Alfred started.

"How did this happen? Where were your damn guards?" he snapped.

Natasha met Mintz's gaze and her chest tightened. Exhaustion lined his weathered face. He'd cleaned up but although soot and mud came off easily with water, worry didn't.

Mintz knew what she knew. The suicide truck hadn't been the real threat.

"Dylan—" Mintz's worn, rough voice cracked.

She held up her hand. It would be better coming from her. Then Dylan could focus his blame on her, not his friend. He was going to need Alfred to help him get through this.

She didn't have the emotional investment that Mintz had in Dylan or Ben. The sting behind her eyelids tried to belie that thought, but she ignored it.

"Dylan, look at me." Her voice wavered.

His intense blue gaze snapped to hers, sending that ripple of shock and awareness through her. She was beginning to expect it, but she wasn't sure she'd ever get used to it.

She touched his forearm. The muscles under his skin stretched taut as steel bands. "Dylan. Whoever did this is long gone by now. All of this is a message."

Dylan scowled at her and jerked his arm out of her grasp. "What the hell are you talking about? What message?"

"Whoever sent that truck and broke into the compound is telling us he can get to Ben any time he wants."

Dylan turned to Mintz. "Alfred, tell her that's not true," he said. "I've got the best security money can buy. Now that we know someone's targeting us, we'll be prepared. Hire more guards. All I need is one more week. Maybe less."

"Dylan—the door was *unlocked*." Mintz's voice was gravelly with emotion. "Whoever did this knows a lot about the layout of the house."

Natasha took a deep breath. "Mintz is right. They had to have access to the house. Ben is not safe here." She looked at Dylan. "You've got a traitor on the inside."

Chapter Five

Dylan's face drained of color as he absorbed the truth of what she was saying.

Witnessing his horrified anguish and his fear of his son's life, Natasha wanted to cry, but she was an FBI agent. FBI agents didn't cry.

"You and Ben have to leave right now," she said.

"That's not going to happen." Dylan glared at Alfred and Natasha.

The two of them exchanged a glance, which only upped Dylan's anger.

"You just want me to drop everything and leave? I don't suppose either of you have a plan for moving the prototype interface." He didn't even pause for an answer. "That's what I thought. You know it can't be moved. We're at a critical point. It's not completely assembled. All the microfibers are exposed. If we try to move it, they could be damaged or broken. I could lose a week, maybe more, just repairing the damage." He shook his head.

"Ben doesn't have a week to spare. I don't care what you do or what it costs, buy me time. Call NSA, the FBI. Get us enough protection that this doesn't happen again."

Alfred nodded. "We've got to address the inside security, too."

"I can't believe there's a traitor on my staff. Who could it be?"

"We'll know soon enough," Alfred muttered. "Okay. I'll review everyone's work history and question them on their whereabouts tonight. We need to go over the telephone logs and view all the security disks, too."

"Hours of work," Dylan said.

Alfred looked at Natasha. "What if we pull your two agents inside? They can review the disks and telephone logs. Plus, knowing that the FBI is on-site might slow down our traitor."

"I think that's a good idea," she said.

Dylan nodded his agreement. "Get them right on it. If I've got a traitor on the inside, I want to know it *now!*"

Alfred started around the orange tape, speaking into his mobile radio.

Dylan moved toward the door. "Natasha, come with me."

"Dylan," Alfred called. "Not that way. We're processing the stairwell for any possible trace evidence."

"Is Campbell in the lab?"

"No. That whole area is sealed off until we test the stairwell."

More time lost. "How long?"

Alfred looked at his watch. "Probably no more than an hour."

"Good." He started up the hill to the front entrance.

Natasha fell into step beside him. "What now?" she asked. "You could use that hour's sleep."

"I'll sleep when Ben can walk without braces." He rubbed his burning eyes. "But why don't you grab a nap?"

"I'll sleep when you sleep."

The picture evoked by her words sent a spear of desire through him. He shook it off, disgusted with himself. He didn't have the strength or the time to spare for useless, distracting sexual cravings. "Since we can't get to the lab let's go have breakfast with Ben."

"You go ahead. Ben barely knows me."

"He'll want to see you."

Natasha turned and walked with Dylan through the front doors and across the atrium to the kitchen. She suppressed a yawn. It had been a long night.

Dylan's eyes were red and his face was haggard. But the fire still burned in him—the fire of determination, of obsession. He'd bring that single-minded concentration to anything he did.

Her brain fed her an image that shocked her. It was as if the moment in her room when he'd touched her forearm had morphed into a different universe—a universe where he pulled her close, his hands pressing her body intimately to his and his mouth covering hers in a burning kiss.

Dylan glanced sideways at her and she snapped back to reality. Her cheeks felt warm. She hoped they weren't turning pink.

"Sorry," she said. "What did you say?"

"I asked you how much you trust your fellow agents?"

"I'd trust Storm with my life. I don't know Gambrini, but my boss, Mitch Decker, hired him and I'd trust Decker with my soul."

"That's a lot of trust."

She met his gaze. "Decker saved my life. So did Storm."

He nodded thoughtfully. "How long will it take you to build a tracking system?"

He wasn't going to be happy with her answer. "I could probably get a good detector-tracer in place within twenty-four hours."

"How much will that slow us down?"

"Not much. That's why it takes so long to set up."

"What if you had the whole system?"

"Obviously I can work faster, but there's a point of diminishing returns. Say my jobs were rated highest priority. That means at times, your jobs would grind to a halt." She shrugged. "Plus if Storm and Gambrini are going to be reviewing security disks and checking telephone usage, that will slow the network that much more. It all burns time."

She paused, doing some rapid calculations in her head. "I can set my jobs at high priority, but not highest. That way you can still work without much perceptible slowdown. Unless I run into an unexpected situation, I might be able to get the supertracker in place in eight to ten hours, maybe a little less."

"Fine. I can afford six hours or so."

"First of all, you just cut my estimate by two hours, and second, please promise me that you understand I can't guarantee anything."

His lips compressed into a thin line. "Just make sure nobody gets near my computer model of the interface software—they could wipe out years of work in a few seconds."

"I understand," she said. "Dylan…" She put a hand on his arm, stopping him at the door to the kitchen. She glanced around before she spoke. "I've been thinking about who the inside source could be. I need a rundown of the staff and their schedules."

"I thought you were going to let your partners take care of that."

"I just need an overview."

"Okay. Campbell has weekends off, although lately he's been here 24-7, other than a day off here and there. His mother is not in good health. Charlene takes off every other weekend. The guards have rotating schedules. I couldn't begin to tell you all of those. You'll have to get them from Alfred."

"Charlene and Campbell don't leave the estate except on their weekends off?"

"Sure, sometimes. They can go shopping, to doctors' appointments, whatever. Campbell can pretty much come and go as he pleases. Charlene has to get someone to watch Ben."

Natasha nodded. "Good. Thanks."

He pushed through the door to the kitchen. She slipped through behind him.

"Daddy!" Ben's face lit up like a star going nova. He squirmed in his toddler chair.

Dylan's face mirrored his son's delight. "Hey, sport," he said, smiling. "What's for breakfast?"

"Daddy, look! Pancakes!" Ben grinned and held up his spoon, which dripped with syrup.

Natasha chuckled. Ben's face and hands were stickier than the plate.

Charlene, who'd been sitting beside Ben, got up and moved down a seat. Dylan nodded his thanks and sat next to his son. "Can I have a syrup kiss?"

Ben dropped his spoon onto his plate with a clatter and reached for his daddy. Dylan scooped him up and hugged him. Ben rubbed his sticky mouth against his daddy's cheek.

"Eww—you're all sticky!" Dylan laughed.

"Eww—you're pricky!" Ben giggled as he rubbed his palm over Dylan's chin and cheek. "Lotsa pricky!"

"Then I guess we're even." Dylan sat and propped Ben on his leg.

It was obvious this was a morning tradition for the two. Natasha felt a hollow ache inside her. She hardly remembered her parents. Certainly not any private loving rituals or jokes. And although there had been certain rituals in some of the foster homes she'd been in, those hardly qualified as loving.

As heartwarming as Dylan's exchange with his son was, it was private—between the two of them. She felt like a voyeur.

Ben turned his sticky grin to her. "Good morning, Tasha!" he cried as Dylan handed him his spoon.

Surprised that he remembered her name, Natasha smiled. "Hi, Ben."

"Look, Tasha, pancakes! You like pancakes?"

"Sure I do. They look good." Above Ben's head

she caught Dylan's eye. He smiled and nodded toward a chair.

She couldn't get over how his smile transformed his drawn features. Even with a day's stubble of beard, he looked like a dark-haired angel.

"I should get started," she said, gesturing vaguely toward the family quarters. "I have some printouts I can study."

"Sit down. You've got to eat."

"Got to eat, Tasha. So you'll grow."

She laughed. "I'm pretty much grown-up already. But I might eat one—just to keep up my strength."

Ben stuffed a spoonful of pancake soaked in syrup into his mouth. "Daddy says I hafta keep up my strength, too."

"You look very strong to me." She sat just as a plump middle-aged woman appeared with two plates of steaming pancakes.

"We're very strong," he said. "We went through the bushes."

"Yes we did, but we weren't supposed to, were we?"

Ben ducked his head for an instant. "I got orders not to do that anymore."

"Orders, eh?" She chuckled and raised her gaze to Dylan's. He was still smiling, only now it seemed aimed at her. Something sharp and sweet shifted inside her. His beautiful smile was lethal. Her cheeks burned.

"Daddy, I want to sit with Tasha."

Apprehension sent her heart racing and the heat in her cheeks faded. Why did Ben want *her* to sit with him? She'd only held a child once, and that was when she'd carried a scratched and dirty Ben to his father.

Dylan stood, lifting Ben with him, and walked around the table. As he set him in Natasha's lap, he whispered in her ear.

"He's just a little boy. He's not going to hurt you."

She cut him an exasperated glance, and tried to ignore the disturbing, exciting heat of his breath on her ear. Then she put her arm around Ben's little waist and balanced him on her lap. He immediately dug into her plate of pancakes.

"Hey, sport. Leave Natasha some food. I'll see you tonight, okay?"

"Play with me today, Daddy."

"I can't today, sport."

Natasha heard the pain in Dylan's voice.

"But I will soon. I promise." He pressed his lips against Ben's hair.

Natasha held on to Ben tightly as waves of conflicting emotions poured over her. The smell and feel of Dylan so close to her, the unfamiliar and yet comfortable weight of Ben on her lap, and the hollow realization of how much she'd missed, having lost her parents.

"And you…" He touched her shoulder, gave it a gentle squeeze. "Eat."

Charlene had finished her breakfast and was watching them. When Dylan left the room, she wiped her mouth and folded her napkin.

Without acknowledging Natasha, she came around the table. "Let's go, cowboy. We need to get all that sticky syrup off you and start your morning therapy."

"I don't want to."

"I know. But remember what your daddy said?"

Ben dropped his spoon with a clatter and crossed his little arms.

"Ben?" Charlene stood over him, her fists propped on her hips.

"He said I gotta be strong."

"Go on, Ben," Natasha murmured. "Do what Charlene says." She didn't look up but she nevertheless felt the daggers Charlene's eyes shot at her.

"Where'd Daddy go? I want Daddy." His voice was about to crack.

"Hey, Ben." Natasha bent enough to look Ben in the eye. "Can I have a syrup kiss?"

The toddler tried to keep frowning, but then his mouth quirked up. "Okay." He leaned over and put his syrupy mouth against her cheek.

"Eww," she said. "Sticky."

Ben giggled. "Eww, softy."

Laughter bubbled up from Natasha's chest. "I didn't know you were such a flirt, Ben." She kissed his syrup-smeared cheek. "You're going to be a lady-killer—just like your dad."

Charlene sniffed.

"Go with Charlene," Natasha whispered. "I'll check on you later, okay?"

Ben leaned close to her ear. "Okay."

AFTER A QUICK shower, Natasha pulled her damp hair back into a ponytail and headed down to the lab. She spent an hour studying the schematic of Dylan's system, testing and re-testing to be sure her hardware tied in with his seamlessly.

Across the hall, Dylan was working on the interface. About the time she stood to do a couple of stretching exercises, Campbell walked into Dylan's office, sending an interested look and a smile in her direction.

The contrast between him and Dylan was obvious even through two glass walls. Dylan's shoulders were bowed with exhaustion. His hair was tousled where he'd run his fingers through it.

Campbell on the other hand looked rested, freshly showered and generally pleased with himself. She had the feeling he spent a lot of time being pleased with himself.

She thought about the other night, when he'd met Dylan and her in the stairwell. He'd looked like hell then. And he hadn't shown up at all when the suicide truck crashed into the front gate. She made a mental note to ask Dylan about him.

She sat and started to work on her tracking program. NSA had set up a state-of-the-art firewall on Dylan's system. According to the log, their spam-blocker was stopping 99.37 percent of all ad-ware robot programs.

The first thing Natasha did was set an alert to capture every single attempt to hit Dylan's system. NSA might be capable of stopping *virtually* all bots, but she wanted to catch one hundred percent of them. She didn't want to take the chance that the hacker might disguise a virus as a harmless advertising bot.

She had no doubt that her program would be better than NSA's. After all, she'd helped to train many of their programmers.

She glanced at the computer's clock as she massaged the back of her neck. She'd been working for over three hours. Her cramped fingers and stiff muscles confirmed that. She arched her back and stretched her arms.

A flurry of activity caught the edge of her

vision. Across the hall, Campbell had kicked his computer chair back against the wall and was pacing, his fingers digging into his scalp.

Dylan said something to him. Campbell glared at him and shook his head violently. He made a fist and aimed it at the glass wall in front of him. Dylan was up and across the room in a split second. He grabbed Campbell's arm, talking intensely.

After a few seconds, Campbell nodded, although his face was still distorted with anger. He grabbed the water bottle that always sat next to him and stalked out of the room.

Dylan wiped his face and turned back toward his workstation. Then he looked up and caught her eye.

Busted. Averting her gaze would only make her look like what she was—an eavesdropper. So she raised her eyebrows in a silent question.

Dylan looked at his hand that still held the stylus, set it down and disappeared through a door on the west wall of his workroom.

Before she could blink, he was standing in her doorway, arms crossed, leaning against the door facing.

She jumped. "You're going to have to show me that secret passage one of these days."

He smiled wearily. "No problem."

He'd showered and shaved. His hair was slightly damp and he had on a white T-shirt and faded jeans. Her eyes lingered on the metal zipper of the jeans for a couple of seconds too long.

"Um—what's the matter with Campbell?" She forced her gaze back to her computer screen.

"He's been searching for that error he swears is the last one. He can't find it. His nerves are shot, just like everybody else's."

"Where'd he go?"

"He said he was going to take a shower."

"Let me take a look at the program."

"That's what I just said to him."

"That's what had him so upset?"

Dylan nodded. "You have to understand. He's been working with me on this for over a year. The area he's looking at is at least fifty thousand lines of code. He said it would take you several days just to get up to speed with the program. He doesn't think we can afford the time."

"And you agree with him?"

"I don't know."

She shook her head. "I don't have to see the whole fifty thousand lines of code. Just the section he's isolated as the source of the bug."

"Look, I'm no programmer, but from what he told me, even the best would need at least twelve hours of review to distinguish good code from bad."

"I *am* the best." She sat back in the ergonomic chair and gazed up at him. "And I can promise you it won't take me that long. I've never met a bug I couldn't squash."

He laughed softly.

The sound coaxed a smile to her face.

"I'll get him to show it to you."

"Dylan, you know in general what Campbell is doing. Show me now." She stood.

"I don't know."

"I'm ready to work now. I guarantee you anything he can do, I can do—probably better."

"You're pretty confident, aren't you?"

"I know what I can do." She paused for an instant. "How well do you know him anyway?"

Dylan's gaze sharpened. "Pretty darn well. Why?"

"You seemed suspicious when he came out of the computer room Tuesday night."

Her comment had caught him off guard. She watched as his mind went back over that moment.

"Not suspicious really. I was surprised. When I left the lab around 2:00 a.m., he promised to lock up in a few minutes. Said he wanted to check a section of code one more time."

"Then we came down at around four o'clock."

"He should have been in bed."

"If *you* quit at two, why did he stay two more

hours? He doesn't strike me as the obsessive type—especially in comparison with you. Plus he looked like he'd been in a tussle."

Dylan nodded grimly. "I noticed that." He straightened. "Come on. I'll show you the code. If you can make sense out of it, great."

Natasha followed Dylan across the hall and into the virtual surgery lab.

Natasha studied the room. Sure enough, as she'd already figured out, Dylan's computer was set up to work with an electronic drawing pad and stylus. On the monitor was a 3-D conceptual graphic of a human spinal cord, with its spaghetti-like tangle of nerves and muscle fibers.

She walked over to Campbell's computer. A streaming matrix of code filled the screen. "Is this the section where he found the bug?"

Dylan stood just behind her. "Probably. Like I told you, the machine code means nothing to me. He said he'd isolated the area."

"Okay, great. Let me figure out where this is and find the same area on my computer. Do I have full access?"

Dylan nodded. "I made sure he took care of that first thing this morning. All you have to do is sign on, place your right thumb on the fingerprint reader then enter the current number from your pass code generator."

Natasha looked at her thumb. "Is it always the thumbprint?"

Dylan shook his head. "With Alfred in charge? He has a rotating system. Everyone has to change fingers at random intervals. If anyone uses the wrong finger or the wrong pass code twice in a row, the system locks down."

Locks down. She suppressed a shudder. "What does lockdown consist of?"

"You saw it in the family wing. Every door slams shut. Only the four master pass codes can reverse lockdown, and then not for at least an hour, depending on the area."

"What if someone's trapped in a locked-down area?"

"Alfred has notifications on all computer monitors and over a loudspeaker system, giving a fifteen-to-thirty-second warning. I told you, he likes triple redundancy."

"But what if someone screws up the pass code or uses the wrong finger accidentally?"

"That's why Alfred built in a second try." He smiled and raised his brows.

She shook her head. "Two tries. Good thing nobody ever gets nervous and misses a number."

"Don't worry. We'll save you if you get locked in."

Doing her best not to give in to the fear his

words invoked, she sucked in a lungful of cool air and sat in Campbell's chair.

She had to force her mind to stop flashing images of doors slamming, latches clunking shut, walls closing in.

She deliberately studied the section of code on his screen, jotting down certain unusual strings of numbers.

Dylan leaned over, his hand on the back of her chair. The scent of soap and cinnamon mouth-wash filled her head.

"So can you tell anything about it?" he asked softly.

"It appears to be part of your virtual surgery program." It took all her concentration to stay on subject. All she wanted to do was turn and rub her cheek against Dylan's, to glean even a small portion of the love he lavished on his little boy.

"How did you come to hire Campbell?" she murmured.

"This program was developed by NSA. He interned with them during his college years. Came with excellent references."

"When was that?" She knew he hadn't been in any of her classes at NSA.

"Probably four or five years ago."

Before her time. She'd started participating in NSA computer training around two years ago.

"So if NSA liked him that much, why didn't they keep him?"

"Think about it. He's hardly their type. Besides, he told me he didn't want a nine-to-five job."

"So instead he's working twenty-hour days for you."

Dylan chuckled, and his soft breath wafted across her cheek, reminding her of just how close he was.

"I suppose he likes to think he's a colleague, not an employee."

"Is he a colleague? How much do you trust him?"

"He's got full access to the program that will save my son's legs. I have to trust him. I have to trust someone."

Natasha heard the desperate note in his voice. "But you're not sure."

She turned her head and realized she was way too close to him. His gaze flickered down to her mouth.

Her pulse leaped as his hot blue eyes and warm breath heated her skin.

"We're talking about my son. I don't trust anyone absolutely."

"Except Alfred."

His gaze met hers. "Except Alfred."

Natasha's pulse fluttered in her throat. She was about to say something she'd never said to anyone. "You can trust me."

His eyes softened and the lines on his forehead relaxed. "I believe you." He raised a hand, hesitated for a microsecond, then pushed a few strands of her hair back behind her ear. His fingertips skimmed the edge of the scratch on her cheek.

"You were injured protecting Ben."

She closed her eyes, reveling in the feel of his fingers on her skin. His breath warmed her cheek and she imagined that it was his lips and not his fingertips that feathered across her skin.

She'd never liked cinnamon that much, but the clean, spicy scent that surrounded her made her mouth water. Though it was more likely the proximity of his lips than the scent that was affecting her. Because the sensation swirled through her and centered at her deepest core.

Then cool air fanned her heated skin. She opened her eyes to find that he'd straightened, frowning.

Embarrassed, she scooted her chair back. "I'm going to—"

"I'll just—"

They both spoke at the same time. Dylan backed up a step and she saw his throat move as he swallowed.

Natasha prayed that she could keep her voice steady. "I'm going to print this screen, so I can find the area from my computer. If there's an error here, I'll get it."

He nodded, still frowning. Then he blinked and moved across the room to his virtual surgery model.

"Great," he said shortly. He sat and picked up the pad and stylus.

After retrieving the printout, Natasha turned. "I'll work on this in my office."

Dylan nodded without looking up. His cheeks were stained a faint pink.

Just like hers. She knew because her face felt hot.

She needed to get out of there, away from his intensity. She had to think logically, analytically, and that was becoming more and more difficult when she was close to Dylan. She reached for the doorknob.

"Wait," he said, standing and pushing his chair back. "Come with me. I'll show you the 'secret passage.'"

She stared at him. "Seriously? There really is one?"

He stepped over to a door on the east wall of the room. She followed him through. On the left as she entered was a door—a heavy steel door.

Dylan used the fingerprint reader and the pass code device to open it.

"I'm sure Alfred told you there are only four people who are allowed access to certain areas? This is one of those areas."

He opened the door. Inside was dark, but as they stepped in, lights came on, projecting a weak beam onto the walls and floor of a tiny alcove.

As the door eased shut behind her, panic tried to crawl up her throat. She looked frantically around the walls, ceiling and floor. A second steel door was in front of her, and to her right her shoulder nearly brushed against a solid wall. To her left was a long dark corridor.

"From the inside, these doors open like fire doors—just push the panic bar."

Dylan's voice surrounded her in the close space. There was barely enough room for the two of them to stand shoulder to shoulder between the doors. Her throat tightened and alarm burned her scalp. "What is this?" She was afraid she knew.

"An escape tunnel. I told you Alfred likes triple redundancy."

"Triple—"

"From the lab there are three exits. Only Alfred, Charlene, me and now you, know about this one. The other two are the main exit via the elevators, and the back stairs that lead to the living quarters."

"So that's why you have the back stairs. I wondered, because they make the family wing much more vulnerable.

"I had to have a fail-safe escape route for Ben. Alfred designed the security system."

They emerged into a glass-walled room next to her office.

Natasha took a deep breath, thankful to be out of that tight dark space. She thought about what Mitch had said, and about the psychiatrist's concern that she wasn't ready for fieldwork because of her claustrophobia.

She'd been confident she could handle it, but now, still shaken from her reaction to the dark tunnel, the question dug at her gut. *Could she if she had to?*

"I could," she murmured.

"What?" Dylan glanced over his shoulder at her as he opened the door to her office.

Had she spoken aloud? "Nothing. How long is the corridor and where does it lead?"

"Long enough. And you wouldn't know the place. It's an abandoned shack on an abandoned road. What you need to know is that there's an old Toyota hidden thirty feet south of the exit, and a key for it above the exit door. Inside the car is a cell phone with a battery pack and directions to the nearest police office."

He turned to her, the blue fire in his eyes bright and hot. "If anything happens, priority one is to get Ben to safety."

"Of course." She knew that Dylan was counting on her. His single-minded resolve to protect his son was fast becoming her top priority, as well. She could brave anything, even the dark tunnel, if it meant keeping Ben safe.

"Dylan, I need to know everything. And Storm and Gambrini need to know where the tunnel is and how to get to it. Is there access to the tunnel from outside?"

"I can print out a map for you that shows the tunnel exit, the vehicle and the fastest route to town."

She frowned as a chill ran up her spine. "That information is in your system? Where?"

Dylan looked stricken.

She grabbed his arm. "Please tell me it's in the encrypted area with the interface program."

He wiped a hand down his face, a hand that trembled. "It's not."

Chapter Six

"Aha. There you are, Natasha," Tom whispered. He grinned and scooted his chair up closer to his computer screen. "I'd recognize that code anywhere."

After the diversion the night before, he was sure they were all working twice as hard today. He'd been trying to penetrate the secure section of Stryker's system since the truck's explosion.

His plan had gone off without a hitch. He knew from his inside connection that his timing had been perfect. The truck hit. All available manpower went to the front gate. The police were called.

Meanwhile, his accomplice had had plenty of time to plant evidence of a second breach—one that had come uncomfortably close to Stryker's child.

Close enough to scare the crap out of Stryker. The neurosurgeon had redoubled his efforts to finish the computer-generated model of the neural interface. And the code he'd just managed to extract told him that Natasha had created an impenetrable firewall. *She thought.*

He smiled to himself. "If you can build it, Nat, I can break it."

He knew her too well. Granted it had been eight years, but even though technology had advanced, people didn't change as easily. Natasha would still code the same way.

He'd managed to frame her eight years ago by duplicating her signature. He could do it again—this time to gain access to Stryker's program.

And that wasn't all. He'd spent months altering his own way of coding. *Changing his signature.* There probably weren't twenty people in the world who were good enough to do that.

Natasha wouldn't know it was him until it was too late. He shuddered as a thrill arrowed through him.

This was better than sex.

He flexed his fingers and sent them flying over the keyboard. Even if the impossible happened and he was unable to break Stryker's security, his backup plan was ready to go.

One way or another, within a few days he'd have the supersoldier technology.

SHE FELL, CRASHING to the ground, the impact knocking the breath out of her. She looked up just as the rifle bullet slammed into her shoulder. Pain split her in two, stole her sight for an instant. She lifted her weapon with one hand and pulled the trigger.

A horrible rumbling filled her ears as her world turned black. She struggled to move, but she was crushed between the cold dirt under her and the suffocating debris on top of her. She couldn't breathe. Couldn't see.

She was buried alive.

Natasha gasped and sat up. Her heart was racing, her pulse throbbed in her temple. She panted, trying to control her breathing as sweat trickled between her breasts.

What was it with the nightmares? She hadn't had dreams like this since childhood. Obviously the stuffy, close bedroom was feeding into her deepest fears. She exercised the breathing techniques she'd learned to combat her claustrophobia.

After a few seconds her heart rate returned to normal and the sweating subsided. But she knew it would be an hour or more before she could go back to sleep.

She grabbed her fanny pack and slipped out her door and down the hall. She pressed her thumb against the reader and entered the current pass code. The lock clicked softly in the silence.

In the atrium, she raised her face to the skylight and took a full, deep breath. Then she lifted her hair off her neck. The knots of tension in her shoulders and back began to relax. The pounding in her temples faded.

"Agent Rudolph? Everything all right?"

Natasha turned toward the quiet voice. "Hector. I'm just getting a breath of air."

"Yes, ma'am." His gaze boldly raked her from head to toe. She had on a pink camisole top and long drawstring pajama pants, but Hector's blatant stare made her feel undressed.

She turned her back on him and headed for the main entrance. As she approached, a middle-aged guard she didn't know opened the glass doors for her.

"Thanks," she murmured, noticing that he made a note on a logbook as she passed through. "I'll be back in a few minutes. I just need some air."

"Yes, ma'am, Agent Rudolph. I can call a guard to accompany you."

"No. I'm fine."

The covered turnaround in front of the house was brightly lit. The lights lined the paved road all the way out to the massive front gates. The green area right around the house was softly lit with solar lights. But Natasha didn't want lights, she wanted stars. So she walked west along the large circular drive until it curved to the north.

She continued west on the grass, down the hill toward the door that led to the living quarters and the lab.

Across the field and up the hill was where the unknown trespasser had gained entry to the estate. A brand-new, heavier-duty metal fence had been brought in early in the afternoon to re-inforce that section.

She walked a few steps up the hill, eyeing the area where the evidence of the breach had been found. Then she looked up.

The lights off to the east obscured the weaker stars, but she could see the brightest ones. She drew in a lungful of sweet night air. After spending hours searching the computer code and only finding one error then waking up from a nightmare, she was stiff and tired.

After a few minutes of indulgence, she turned her attention back to the foliage that hid the fence. Somewhere out there beyond it either Storm or Gambrini was on duty. One of them was working security while the other was helping with the questioning and background checks of Dylan's staff. She pulled her wrist-COM unit from her fanny pack and spoke into it quietly.

"Rudolph here. Storm?"

"Hey, Nat."

"Where are you?"

"Bored to death in Guardhouse Alpha."

Natasha smothered a chuckle. "Guardhouse Alpha?"

"Yeah. In case you haven't noticed, Sergeant Mintz is a born and bred military type."

"I noticed. What do you think about his security?"

Storm paused. "Top-notch. What I don't get is what's the point? I understand the No Such Agency offered Stryker ironclad security in one of their supersecret facilities."

"You'd have to know him. He doesn't trust anyone else to protect his child."

"So *you* know him?" Storm drawled.

"Stop it, Storm. Not everything is about sex."

Despite Storm's implication, she considered his words. Did she know Dylan? During the few days she'd been here, she'd come to respect his expertise. She'd begun to share his obsession with keeping Ben safe. If Ben were her child, she'd die for him.

"Who said anything about sex?" Storm chuckled.

"Never mind." She sighed, a tiny smile tugging at her lips.

"Yeah, let's change the subject. Where are you? In bed? Whatcha wearing?"

"Nice segue, Mr. One-Track-Mind. Am I going to have to kick your butt again?"

"Again?" Storm laughed. "You haven't kicked it the first time. Although I'd be happy to let you see what you can do." He paused. "Sorry, sugar. I can't help it. It's lonely in Guardhouse Alpha."

"Maybe you should take advantage of the time alone and work on your social skills."

Storm laughed.

"Okay, Storm. Listen. My COM unit doesn't work inside the house," she told him. "Neither do cell phones. When you get the photo-analysis of the fibers caught on the fence, call me on the landline or send me a message through Mintz."

"You got it, sugar."

"So has Mintz briefed you on the layout of the house and grounds?"

"Yep. We know where everybody sleeps. We have a blueprint of the entire estate. We're set."

"Did he show you *absolutely* everything—including all the exits?" Natasha said carefully. She knew better than to assume their channel was totally secure.

"He sure did. All of 'em."

"Good. Stay safe out there. I'm out." She turned off the COM unit and stuck it back in her fanny pack.

She'd wandered up the hill while talking to Storm. Above her head, a quarter moon shone brightly. Natasha took another refreshing breath of cool night air and curled her toes in her thong sandals, shivering as the cool dampness of the dew spilled onto her toes.

A twig snapped behind her.

She laid her hand on her fanny pack and slid open the nearly silent zipper.

The crunch of leaves had her whirling, slapping at her fanny pack.

"Hey!" Strong hands gripped her upper arms. "Whoa. It's me, Dylan. What are you doing out here?"

She pulled away from his grip. Had he heard her exchange with Storm?

"It was stuffy in my room. I wanted some air. And I spoke to Special Agent Storm for a moment." She frowned at him. "Did you come out here looking for me?"

Dylan shook his head. "I had to get out of the lab for a while. It's nice out here tonight." He looked up at the sky. The moon was bright, sending faint shadows across the ground and sprinkling pale gold glitter on Natasha's hair.

It floated across her shoulders, making his fingers itch to touch it, to capture it between his hands and bury his nose in it. He took in her slender, sturdy body, encased in the sheer pink material of her pajamas. The delicate bones of her shoulders and her slender, muscled arms made his mouth water and his body ache.

He ran a hand down his face. He was more exhausted than he'd realized. He was drifting off into dreamland while standing upright.

Natasha angled her head at him. "You're so tired you're falling asleep standing up."

Not falling asleep, he thought. Daydreaming certainly.

"I don't think you've slept since I've been here," she continued.

"I've caught a few naps with Ben. Knowing he's right there, beside me…" He shrugged.

Natasha's face softened. "He's such a sweet little boy."

"Don't let him fool you. He can be a handful." His voice nearly cracked. He looked away, toward the fence. "So how's the hacker-tracking going?"

"I was going to find you before I went to bed, but Campbell told me you were with Ben. I've set traps and traces on your system to alert us if anyone tries to hack in. I've also put an extra layer of security on e-mail. There's a three-layer system of sign-ons now, including the computer-generated pass codes. We've got to keep the hacker out of the secure area. Keep him from injecting a worm or breaking the encryption."

Dylan listened to Natasha's low voice in fascination. She seemed so young, but she was so confident, so smart, so irresistible.

As soon as the thought hit his brain, he rejected it. He wasn't interested in her or anyone else. He had only one goal—saving his son's legs.

"Sounds good. What's your impression of the hacker?"

She sent him a sidelong glance. "He's very good. Scarily good."

He nodded. "I know. Whoever this is has already managed to do more than NSA thought anyone would be able to. And those guys aren't often wrong. So he's got to be the best."

Natasha didn't comment.

He heard something. He couldn't identify it. In fact it was so faint that it might have been an animal moving about in the woods. Still…

"Let's go back to the house." The breeze had picked up. It swirled her bright hair around her face and shoulders, and he thought he saw her shiver.

Was she chilly, or had she heard the sound, too? He didn't like the idea of her being beyond his narrow circle of protection.

She looked past him toward the house and for a second her eyes glimmered as if with fear. It was the second time he had the feeling she didn't like being in his house.

"Are you okay?" he asked, just as a flash of light hit his dark-adapted eyes and a loud crack echoed around him.

"Natasha!" he cried as a second flash blinded him.

"Get down!" she shouted.

Her pale skin and bright hair made her stand out like an angel in the darkness. Adrenaline, hot as lava, pumped through his veins as the fight-or-flight instinct drove him.

He lunged for her just as a third flash threw the field into garish light and shadow. He hit her body with enough force to take her to the ground, then he rolled on top of her.

The next flash was accompanied by a deep thud. He cringed. His pulse hammered. He spread his body over hers, shielding her. His chest was pressed against her back and his groin rubbed against her bottom.

Doing his best to ignore the signals his body was sending to his brain, he wrapped her head in the circle of his arms and lowered his head beside hers. Her mouth was pressed against his cheek and his brushed her ear.

"Roman c-candles!" Natasha whispered breathlessly, just as his mobile radio crackled.

Without changing position, he reached for the radio. "Alfred, what's going on?"

"Fireworks. I'm sending the guard in Beta to find whoever's setting them off and stop them."

"Thanks." He thumbed the radio off and clipped it back onto his belt in one quick motion.

Beneath him, Natasha wriggled. Her movements played havoc with his efforts at control. The feel of her bottom moving against him was torture. He felt himself growing hard.

He was caught between a rock and a very hard place. Her wriggling had aroused him.

Hell, it probably wasn't just her. It was the combination of surprise, danger, darkness and the feel of soft, firm woman—something he hadn't indulged in, had hardly thought about, for the past three years.

He rolled off her. She immediately turned over, and he met her furious gaze. Her green eyes sparked like fire striking jade.

From her expression, it was obvious that he hadn't moved away fast enough. She'd felt his arousal.

She jumped up and planted her feet apart directly in front of him and propped her fists on her hips. The moonlight revealed the spots of pink high on her cheekbones.

"What the hell was that?" she snapped.

That. He almost laughed, knowing she wasn't talking about what he was thinking about. He stood, wishing his jeans weren't so formfitting, but it was far too late for that wish to come true.

He felt his face heat up. "Fireworks, according to Alfred."

"I mean throwing me to the ground."

He shrugged. "I thought we were in danger. I was protecting you."

She threw up her hands. "I'm the FBI agent. I'm the trained professional here. Don't you think I should have been protecting you?"

Her hair was a mess. Her face was red, her mouth thin with anger, and her pink pajamas were twisted, revealing the tip of one breast. She was furious and gorgeous and strong and sexy.

He shook his head slowly. "No, I don't."

She slapped her waist. "I have a weapon—" She cursed. "Where's my gun? You knocked it out of my pack when you hit me."

She whirled, scanning the ground, then spotted it a few feet behind them.

She stalked over to pick it up. When she reached down, Dylan saw a dark spot on her top, just below her left shoulder. "What's that?" He touched her arm.

She jerked away. "What? Nothing."

"It's blood. You fell on something, didn't you?" He wrapped his arm around her waist and pulled her closer. When he peeled the stretchy material of her top down an inch or so, he saw the nasty scratch below her shoulder blade.

"No," she said tightly. "I didn't fall. You pushed me." She stepped away again and used the tail of her top to wipe off her gun. "I'm going to check out the source of the fireworks."

"No you're not. You're coming with me. I want to check on Ben, and you need medication for that wound." He grabbed her arms and pulled her toward him.

She let him turn her around. "This is ridiculous," she muttered. "I'm capable of taking care of myself. There's nothing to slathering some alcohol on a scratch. And besides, you had no business throwing me to the ground like that. You could have gotten yourself shot."

"Hey," he said, angling his head to look her in the eye. "I'm a guy. Protecting is what we do."

She looked up and he was surprised to see a different kind of light in her green eyes. She appeared a little stunned, and a tiny smile played across her generous lips. She lowered her gaze, then raised it again, as if trying to make up her mind.

"Thank you," she said softly. "That's nice."

And then she raised her head and kissed his mouth. Her lips were like moth wings—soft, fluttery, warm.

He slid his hand through her hair the way he'd longed to ever since he'd first seen her. Then closed his fist and held her head still as he kissed her—working like hell to keep his kiss as soft and gentle as hers had been.

It took all his control to keep from pressing her to his length and making the kiss a full-body experience. His arm shook with his restraint.

She pulled away and his heart lurched. Her eyes were dewy and heavy-lidded. Had he gone too far too fast?

After a quick searching look, she kissed him again. Again he had no defense.

Her hand ran up his biceps and across his shoulder. She cupped his cheek in her palm as she kept on kissing him.

Suddenly, the utter stupidity of what he was doing hit him. He was kissing a virtual stranger while his home and his child were under attack. He jerked away.

Natasha stood there, frozen for a few seconds, then the red spots returned to her cheekbones and she ducked her head. "I am so sorry," she murmured, and took off for the house.

Dylan stood in place for a moment, cursing himself. He had a baby to worry about. A baby who was running out of time. What the hell had he been thinking?

The answer to that was a no-brainer. He *hadn't* been thinking. He'd been reacting. He'd told her *I'm a guy, it's what we do*. And it was true. Protection. But also sex.

Chapter Seven

Tom looked at the schematic on his computer screen, then back at the device sitting in front of him. He traced each wire one more time, assuring himself that each one was perfectly placed, perfectly aligned. Then he opened a small plastic-wrapped package and carefully removed the gray substance inside. He kneaded it until it was soft and malleable.

After consulting the schematic again, he separated a nice-sized sphere of the gray substance and rolled it between his palms.

It was almost ready. There was only one last bit of construction—the hardest part. For this he needed a cell phone and something to serve as a trigger.

Just then a knock sounded on his front door. Excitement slithered up his spine. Everything was coming together like clockwork.

By the time his accomplice got back to

Stryker's estate this afternoon, everything would be ready.

It was only a matter of time.

NATASHA CLOSED HER EYES and stretched her arms and back. That was the last test. The imposter program was ready.

She glanced at the clock in the lower right of the monitor. Four o'clock on Sunday afternoon. The weekend had passed quietly. Since Charlene was off and Dylan was working night and day on the neural interface program, she and Mintz had shared babysitting duties.

During the hours Mintz was watching Ben, she worked on her imposter program. Finally, by the time Charlene got back Sunday afternoon to relieve them, she'd completed the program.

She ran through the code one last time, paying particular attention to the encryption she'd set up to firewall the bogus neural interface software.

As she scrolled screen by screen, looking for errors, she rubbed her temple where a headache was beginning. She closed her burning eyes for a few seconds.

"Hey, is everything all right?"

Her eyes flew open and her breath hitched. "Oh, Dylan. I'm fine. Sorry. I've looked at this screen so long it's getting blurry."

"You should take a break."

She took in his appearance. He leaned against the door in a supremely masculine slouch. He crossed his arms. A green T-shirt stretched across his shoulders and hung over snugly fitting wheat-colored jeans. His hair was tousled where he'd pushed his fingers through it. He hadn't shaved, and the dark stubble contrasted sharply with his skin.

She was suddenly struck by a memory of his stubble scraping her cheek when they'd kissed the other night. It took tremendous willpower not to touch her cheek. His kiss had been just like him—intense, focused. And she'd had the feeling he was holding back. What would he be like if he let go? If he kissed her with the same passion he brought to everything else he did?

She realized she was staring at his lips. What had he said? Something about a break?

"I'd say you're the one who needs the break."

"I just spent a couple of hours with Ben." His expression softened. "I was hoping he'd want a nap, but no such luck. We played 'Daddy is a big bouncy cushion.'"

Natasha smiled. "I learned that game this weekend, too."

"Thanks for helping watch him. He likes you. He said you were fun. Fun and 'bootiful.'"

"He said that?"

Dylan smiled at the way her face lit up. Ben was right. She was "bootiful." But he should be thinking about the interface—not how beautiful she was.

He stepped around her desk until he could see the monitor. He leaned over and grasped the back of her chair. "What are you working on?"

"I'm building an imposter program on your second server. It should keep the hacker's accomplice from accessing the real server while you finish the interface."

"What good is that going to do?"

He saw her stiffen. She'd heard the skepticism in his voice.

"Like I said, it will divert users to a second server—the shell."

Her hair tickled his nose, sending her fresh strawberry scent rushing through him. Stirring his blood. He clamped his jaw.

"I'm not sure I see the point of this. You're setting it up so the hacker hits this program instead of the real code? If he's good enough to get in, is your imposter going to fool him?"

"No. It won't fool him. He'd know right away if we switched programs on him." She turned her head and suddenly he was too close. Close enough that he could almost taste her lips. So close he could imagine he felt the sweep of her gold-tipped lashes.

He straightened and stepped backward. There

was already a war going on between his heart and his brain as he struggled to balance his need to keep Ben safe with the urgency to finish the interface.

Now the game was complicated by a third player—his libido. It shocked him that he could think about sex while time was running out for his son's legs.

Damn, he wished they'd sent him a male agent.

Natasha said something. He forced his brain to concentrate.

"It's the house computers I'm concerned about. I want to move their hardwiring to the shell server."

"Why?"

She swiveled her chair to face him. "We think someone on the inside is feeding information to the hacker, right? This bogus program is good enough to fool anyone other than an experienced programmer."

"What about e-mail? Ordering supplies?"

"I've synched the e-mail and local databases. Everyone in the house will be working on the shell, not the real server. Each time a file is changed, incoming or outgoing, the change is automatically swept for viruses and worms. Suspicious files will be isolated for me to look at directly. The clean files are updated to the real server every two hours. And hopefully, if the hacker tries to sabotage the system through e-mail, he won't realize he's being screened by the imposter."

Dylan stared at her. "You did all that since Friday, *and* spent what—eight hours with Ben?"

She shrugged. "Playing with Ben was relaxing."

He nodded. He knew what she meant. An hour spent with his son refreshed and rejuvenated him more than a nap.

"So what about the interface?"

"You and Campbell will still work on the real server. Your time is too valuable and there's too much room for error if you have to go through the screening process for everything you do. The hacker will see that some programs have been moved, but that won't surprise him. In fact, he's expecting me to try and stop him. He'd be suspicious if I *didn't* change some programs. But it would take him a couple of hours online to figure out just what I've done, and he can't risk staying online that long." She shrugged. "At least, that's the theory."

"He knows you're here, tracking him."

She sent him a sharp glance, then turned her attention back to the monitor. "He knows someone is. If there really is someone inside the house feeding him information, they've probably told him my name."

"What about you? Do you know who he is?"

"There are thousands of hackers all over the world. Several thousand in the U.S. alone. Of those, probably no more than a hundred have the talent and intelligence to get as far as this guy has."

There was a note in her voice that Dylan didn't like. She sounded guarded, even a little nervous. And her answer was glaringly evasive. He watched her carefully. "You've probably run into all one hundred of them."

"Not all." She fiddled with the mouse.

"But it's likely that whoever this is, you've seen his work before."

"It's possible. I don't know how likely it is." She glanced at her watch, then stood. "I need to get to work on the hardwiring."

He watched her narrowly as she pushed the computer chair neatly up to the desk. She was hiding something. Lying to him. Did she know more about the hacker than she was telling?

"Okay," he said. "So what's next?"

"I need to move the hardwiring to the shell server. How many computers are in the house?"

"Wow, I'm not sure. Let's see." He mentally counted. "Maybe twenty. Alfred can tell you. He has a schematic for the connections."

"Good. What about outside?"

"No outside computers are linked to the server.

The guardhouse computers are self-contained. They operate the gates and run the security cameras. Nothing else."

"Nothing else? Ben's play area?"

"No. There's one right inside the door to the kitchen, though."

"The tunnel?"

He shook his head. "None out there. I think it's wired, though. You'll need to check Alfred's schematic."

Natasha bit her lip and her gaze faltered. "We need to put one out there. It would be better to have it at the—" She paused. "The tunnel exit."

He frowned. He'd seen the same look on her face in the tunnel access room. In fact, he'd seen that look several times before. She was afraid, and he was beginning to figure out why. Either she was terrified of the dark or she was claustrophobic.

"Is something wrong?" he asked.

"No. Nothing." She didn't look at him. "We can't leave any access to the house unguarded."

"You don't have to worry about the tunnel. If an unauthorized person gets in, steel doors close and lock on both ends. They'll be trapped."

Natasha's shoulders tightened visibly.

"It's close spaces, isn't it?"

"What?"

"You're claustrophobic."

She rolled her eyes. "Being trapped by steel doors in a dark tunnel isn't my idea of fun."

He chuckled, letting it go for the moment. "I can agree with that. So now what? Switch the wiring?"

"Where's Campbell?"

"He took today off. Needed to check on his mother."

"Good. I don't want anyone other than Mintz to know about the imposter program."

"Right. We still don't know who's feeding the hacker information."

"I can have the wires switched in a couple of hours," Natasha went on. "Then I need to set up a computer at the tunnel's exit. You said there's a shack at the exit?"

The strain in her voice was unmistakable. His heart went out to her. She could deny it all she wanted, but it was obvious that the tunnel bothered her.

"Yeah. Been abandoned for years."

She nodded, chewing on her lower lip. "So, I'd better get to work."

"Let me know when you're ready to head out through the tunnel. I'll go with you."

She started to say no. He could tell. But then she looked past him, toward the tiny access room.

Near panic froze her features and her face turned pale. She swallowed.

He touched her shoulder. "Natasha?" he whispered.

She closed her eyes briefly, then nodded. "Thanks."

DYLAN SPENT the next hour or so practicing on the virtual surgery model, attaching nerves to minuscule, nearly invisible prosthetic fibers, and timing himself. He had to attach over three thousand nerves, and he had to do it in less than twelve hours. He was afraid to leave Ben under anesthesia longer than that.

He glanced at the computer clock, wondering how close Natasha was to finishing the rewiring of the computers. He stood and stretched, reaching toward the ceiling with his fingers, then flexing them. He walked down the hall to the server room and let himself in.

She was bent over, reaching behind the backup server. Dylan had an excellent view of her curvy bottom in low-rise, faded jeans. Her little T-shirt had ridden up and exposed bare skin from the curve of her hips up to just below her bra strap.

Stop ogling, he admonished himself. His inability to control his libido around her was becoming ridiculous. He usually had no trouble staying focused. And he'd never had a better incentive to dismiss any distractions. So why was she slipping more and more into his thoughts and dreams?

She straightened with a quiet groan and noticed him. "Oh. I didn't hear you come in." She clutched a screwdriver in her right hand.

"Not surprised, with the air conditioners and all the equipment humming." He nodded toward her hand. "Are you done?"

"Just finished. I haven't tested any of the remote computers, but I can do that tonight."

"Are you ready to brave the tunnel?" He smiled.

She didn't. Her lips pressed together and a muscle in her jaw tensed. She took a deep breath and arched her back and neck, then caught her hair in both hands and twisted it up. The action lifted her top and revealed the curve of her waist and her delicately shaped navel. She secured her hair in place with something invisible.

"Okay, yeah. I'm ready." She gestured toward a table with several computers and monitors sitting on it. "That one on the end is ready to go. I've tested it with a short wire hookup to the shell server. You were right. Mintz confirms that the tunnel is already wired."

"Okay. Let's get started." Dylan pulled a large hand truck over and loaded the computer and monitor onto it. He rolled the truck out to the tunnel entrance. After opening the first door, he stepped back.

"You go first. I'll be right behind you with the truck."

Natasha stared at the steel door that led into the tunnel. Ridiculous, unreasoning fear rose like bile in her throat. *Don't let him know how afraid you are.*

Her hand trembled as she pressed her thumb on the fingerprint reader, then entered the current pass code. With a soft click, the heavy door swung open. She stepped into the dark tunnel.

The cart's wheels echoed through the cavernous space.

"How—how long is the tunnel?"

"About three-quarters of a mile."

"Can you turn on some lights?"

Dylan laughed softly. "Take a couple of steps."

Panic flared, squeezing the air from her lungs. She fought to control her breathing. Was Dr. Shay right? Was she not ready to be back in the field? Why had Mitch let her take the assignment if she was this unstable?

She took a step, her breath hitching. Then another. With a quiet thunk, dim lights appeared. They stretched down the seemingly endless tunnel as far as she could see. Her pulse hammered in her ears, so loud she was afraid Dylan heard it.

She didn't want to feel like this, didn't want to be such a coward. But deep inside her she knew that only the sound of the cart's wheels behind her and the thought of letting Dylan down kept her from turning and sprinting back to the door.

She glanced back, her eyes craving more light than the dim bulbs put out. But not even a sliver shone around the edges of the steel door. She couldn't glean any reassurance there.

Dylan's blue eyes narrowed. "You okay?" he asked.

"Yeah, sure."

"You can walk faster if you want. I'll be right behind you."

"I'm fine," she snapped. She never took her eyes off the dim can lights as she walked. After a few moments, she realized she was counting them, and there seemed to be as many in front of her as she'd already passed. She moaned under her breath.

"Natasha, how certain are you that you'll be able to ID the hacker? And how long is it going to take?"

She grimaced in the darkness. Dylan suspected that she knew who was hacking into his system. She'd seen the sharp skepticism in his eyes. But she didn't know—not for sure.

She hadn't told anyone—not even her boss—

her suspicion that Dylan's hacker was the same man who'd framed her for accessing the FBI's terrorist database. It was ironic that instead of sending her to prison, Tom's double cross had turned her life around.

Would anyone believe that she hadn't spoken to him since? That she had no idea where he was or what he'd been doing the past eight years?

No. No one would believe her. She wouldn't, if she were them. She didn't want to say anything until she was sure. She wanted to be wrong.

"I feel like I'm really close," she said.

"You said there were probably only a hundred hackers who could do what he's done so far. But you never answered my question. How many of those hundred or so hackers do you know?" His voice took on a hard edge.

"I've worked for the FBI for eight years. I have two major responsibilities. I spend about half of my time in the field. The rest of the time I chase down hackers, mostly irritating kids who like to release annoying, but harmless virus programs or worms just for fun."

"But sometimes you deal with malicious ones, right? The ones who are working for terrorists, who want to gain access to programs like the interface to sell to the highest bidder."

Natasha was having trouble concentrating on

what Dylan was saying. He'd distracted her for a few seconds with his questions, but now the panic was growing again, clawing its way up her throat like a scream, and his voice was nothing more than a low buzz in her head. She sucked in a lungful of conditioned air and tried to push the panic down, but she heard her breath sawing in and out. She was sure he did, too.

His hand touched her arm. "Look up ahead," he said softly.

"What? Where?" In the far distance, she saw a red glow that stood out among all its pale yellow companions. Wary hope fluttered in her chest. "What's that?"

"The end of the tunnel."

"Oh." She bit her lip as tears of relief filled her eyes. *The end of the tunnel.* Her panic faded, receded like the surf at low tide. She flexed her fingers, and winced when they cramped. She hadn't realized she'd been clenching them.

She'd made it. But she still had to go back. Could she do it again? She glanced over her shoulder.

The narrow passageway stretched as far as she could see. Exactly the same—the same shadows, the same stale cold air—the same laughably dim lights.

She shivered and vowed she'd do her best,

because that's what Dylan expected, and she didn't want to let him down.

Within a couple of minutes they were at the exit door. Just as Dylan had described, the door had a panic bar on the inside. There was barely enough light to see it. She pushed on it with both hands, doing her best to stay calm. This was it. Her heart pounded. There was light on the other side of the door. *You can't break down now,* she lectured herself silently.

The tunnel door opened into a small closet as dark as the tunnel. No! Where was the light? She bit her lip and fought to control her rising panic. Just in front of them was another steel door. She paused, but Dylan didn't say anything, so she pushed its panic bar. As the door swung open, bright sunlight poured in. She breathed in warmth and fresh air, gaining strength with each breath. The fresh air and sun fed her. Finally, she gained the courage to try her shaky legs, actually believing—sort of—that they wouldn't give way on her.

"Wow. This really is an old place, isn't it? Who lived here?" she asked Dylan, wincing at the quaver in her voice.

He pushed the hand truck through the doors. "Who knows? When I bought the property, it included this abandoned house. It sits on an overgrown dirt road. Nobody's driven on that road for years. I was going to have the house torn down, but Alfred wanted to use it to hide the tunnel exit."

She nodded, keeping her back to him, blinking to get rid of the tears that threatened to fall. She cleared her throat. "More of his triple-redundancy."

"Natasha?" He put his hand on her shoulder and gently turned her to face him. "It's okay if you were scared in the tunnel."

"Don't—" She bowed her head. She did not want him to see her with tears in her eyes. What kind of FBI agent cried?

But his fingers touched her chin, lifting it. "What happened to you?"

She shook her head. "Nothing."

She stepped backward, but he didn't let her step away from him. He moved with her, his fingers still brushing her chin. "Tell me."

His low voice rumbled next to her ear, sending waves of awareness through her, calming the panic.

"You're safe here. You can trust me. I'll take care of you."

She pushed his hand away and took a step backward. "I wish you wouldn't say that. Don't you understand? I'm supposed to be the protector. I'm supposed to be taking care of you and Ben."

"You are." His pensive smile made her wonder what he was thinking.

"No I'm not. Look at me. I'm a mess. I'm standing here wishing I could just—" She stopped. There was no sense in going further. She would just embarrass herself more.

"Wishing what?" He pushed a strand of hair off her forehead and ran his fingers across her cheek.

Desire streaked through her, uninvited and yet welcome. She gasped softly.

He cupped her cheeks in his palms and urged her to look at him. He was so close she could feel his breath—she was surrounded by the scent of soap and cinnamon. When she looked up his hot blue gaze traveled from her eyes to her mouth.

"Tell me what frightens you."

She strained against his hands. His intense blue gaze held her in thrall. Her pulse thrummed in her temple, in her throat, all the way through her. "This," she murmured. "You."

He smiled and lowered his head until their foreheads touched. "I'm not talking about right now," he whispered. "Right now I'm nervous, too."

His voice soothed her, calmed her. She closed her eyes, letting herself go in a way she'd never done before.

She was with Dylan. She was safe. His gaze heated her skin, his hands caressed her cheeks and neck. She felt like quicksilver, liquid and shimmering, poised on the very edge of release.

"Tell me what frightens you when you lie in bed at night. When you're alone in the dark."

His words evoked fear, and the fear tried to drive away the liquid feeling. She put her hands on his chest, pushing, but he resisted. He slid his palms over her shoulders and down to her waist. He wrapped her in his strong embrace.

"Don't ask me that," she pleaded, laying her head on his chest. Her lips moved against the soft material of his T-shirt. He cradled her head in one hand and pressed his mouth against her hair.

"I'll tell you what I'm afraid of. I'm afraid to sleep," he whispered hoarsely. "I'm afraid I'll wake up and find out my nightmares are the reality and that all this—this is the dream."

His words were heartbreaking. His voice was hushed and tight. She squeezed her eyes shut and tried to speak past the ache in her heart. "What are your nightmares?" she asked.

His muscles tensed around her. His voice was muffled by her hair. "I dream I'm alone, buried in my basement like some deranged hermit, obsessed with healing my son. But I can't, because Ben's not here. He—he died that day, in the car with his mother."

His shattered voice broke her heart—ripped it

open. She leaned back in his arms and looked up at him. "It's just a nightmare. He's alive. He loves you more than anything in the world."

He gave her a sad smile and nodded. "In the middle of the night it's easy to believe the nightmare."

"I know." Natasha swallowed against the tears that clogged her throat. He'd told her his private fears. Could she tell him hers? Would it help either of them if he knew what terrified her?

"Why are you afraid of the dark, Tasha?"

She closed her eyes and buried her nose in the hollow of his shoulder. "My parents were diplomats. They were killed in a car bombing in Kosovo when I was six. Collateral damage. I was in the backseat. They were in the front. A soldier must have heard me crying in the wreckage. I hardly remember it."

Dylan winced at her words. In the backseat, just like Ben. A lot of things started to make sense to him. Her frustration at the lack of windows in the family quarters. Her unease when she first saw the underground lab. Her immediate connection with his son.

"It was a long time before anyone found me. I don't know how long. I think I knew my parents were dead. I remember a soldier looking through the broken car window, telling me not to cry.

Telling me he'd take care of me." Her shoulder twitched in a half shrug. "I don't remember much after that, until I was brought back to the U.S. and placed in foster care."

"But you dream about it," he said, his throat clogged with sadness for the little girl she'd been.

She nodded. "I'm trapped in the dark," she said in a small voice. "I can't move. And nobody comes to save me."

Dylan felt her trembling, felt her shuddering breaths. He wrapped his arms more tightly around her. "But they did come to save you, and you're here now. And you're strong and brave and beautiful."

Her eyes softened to a velvety green. "Thank you."

He smiled. "For what? Stating the obvious?"

"No. For trusting me."

He frowned as her words echoed in his brain. Did he trust her? He realized he did. She'd been right beside him each time danger had threatened. She'd protected Ben without thought to her own safety.

A tendril of her hair slipped out of its restraint. He caught it. Then he ran his fingers through her hair and whatever held it let go. It tumbled her blond waves to her shoulders.

He cupped her cheek in his palm again and kissed her lips. The feel of her mouth under his sent desire streaking straight to his groin. He wanted her with a ferocity that he couldn't remember ever feeling before.

She pulled back slightly, but he held her head still and dipped his head to kiss her again. This time she angled her head and her lips moved under his.

When he took the kiss deeper, she followed, parting her lips and letting him in. Kissing him back.

He slid his hand down her back and encountered warm bare skin. Pressing her close, he let her feel how much he wanted her.

She froze for an instant, but his mouth and hands coaxed her across the line of trepidation. As her body lost its tension and became supple and lithe, they melded together.

He trailed soft kisses across the smooth sweet skin of her cheeks, her jaw, her neck. The scent of strawberries clouded his senses. He moved back to her mouth.

She met him, kissed him, ran her fingers up his shoulders to his neck.

Somewhere, outside of him, a bothersome noise erupted.

She stiffened.

"It's okay," he whispered against her mouth as the noise continued, and the real world started to intrude on his seductive haze.

"Dylan—" She pulled away enough to meet his gaze. "The telephone."

Phone. He straightened, fighting the haze of desire. The tunnel-house phone had its own exchange. The caller had to be Alfred. No one else knew they'd come out here.

He let go of her and grabbed the handset.

"Alfred?"

"Dylan, aren't you done yet?"

Alfred's crisp, slightly disapproving tone catapulted Dylan back to the present—to now. To the reality of what they were supposed to be doing. His face burned in humiliation.

"Just about," he snapped, raking his hair back and wincing at her familiar scent that clung to his fingers.

What the hell was wrong with him? How could he have allowed himself even a second of self-indulgent fantasy when every minute that passed brought Ben closer to the point of no return?

"Did you need something, Alfred?"

"Campbell's back. Thought you'd want to know. He's in his room now, but he'll be heading down to the lab soon."

"Thanks."

"Dylan?"

"What?" He knew he was acting like a grouch, and he knew why. He was pissed at himself *and* at Natasha. One of them should have had better sense. Hell, he couldn't blame her. He was the one that had started it all.

"Is everything okay out there?"

"Just fine. Keep Campbell away from the lab for—" He turned and raised his eyebrows at Natasha.

She'd already started hooking up the computer. Her cheeks were bright pink, but she acted as if everything was normal.

"Five minutes here," she said shortly.

"—fifteen minutes. Give us time to get back through the tunnel. I don't want him to know we've been out here."

"Will do. Tell Agent Rudolph that the FBI confirmed that the fibers on the fence were planted. At least two edges were cut."

"Planted? What does that mean?"

"It means someone wanted us to believe that whoever left footprints outside the west door came in through the fence. It's obvious that they came from the house, but we're checking the area around the fence. I'm out."

As Dylan hung up the phone, Natasha planted her fists on her hips. "What was planted?"

He looked at her. "The fibers on the fence. Your FBI lab confirmed they were planted. Alfred said two sides were cut, not torn."

"I knew it. I'll let Storm know to check for footprints at the fence, see if they're a match for the garden boots." She nodded and went back to hooking up the computer.

He watched her, not knowing what to say. He was furious at himself for using up precious minutes of Ben's time indulging himself.

But as hard as he tried, he couldn't be totally sorry for what he'd done. He understood Natasha a lot better now. Now that she'd told him what had happened to her as a child.

And to his surprise, he'd told her about his nightmares—something he'd never told anyone. But it felt right for her to know.

He helped her with the setup. Neither of them said an unnecessary word as Natasha made sure the PC was running and synching correctly with both the shell server and the real one.

"All done," she said.

"Great. I'll get Alfred to come and get the cart. Let's get back to the lab. Campbell's back and if you don't want anyone to know about this computer, we need to be out of the access room before he comes downstairs."

She nodded and followed him back through the doors to the tunnel. They walked the length without saying a word.

As they emerged from the tunnel access

room, Dylan saw Campbell bent over Natasha's workstation.

He glanced at Natasha. She saw him, too. They slipped across the hall and through the door to her office.

"Jerry? What's going on?" Dylan snapped.

Campbell straightened and glared at Dylan, then at Natasha. "That's what I want to know. What the hell do you think you're doing?"

Chapter Eight

"What are *you* doing in Natasha's office, Jerry?"

Campbell took a step toward Natasha. "Ask her what she's—"

"Jerry—" Dylan stepped between him and Natasha. "Calm down. I'm asking you."

Campbell's fists were clenched at his sides. He glared at Natasha, but then he took a deep breath. "I came down to let you know I was back and to see if there was anything I needed to do this evening," Campbell retorted. "I found the lab empty, so I checked the computers. And found this."

Dylan glanced at Natasha's monitor. "Look, Campbell, I don't know what you saw, but—"

"What I *see* is that she's rerouted the system through a different server." He rounded on Natasha. "You can't go messing around with the system. What the hell did you think you were accomplishing?"

Dylan grabbed his arm. "Calm down, Jerry. What's the problem? You know Natasha's here to stop the hacker."

Campbell laughed. "By setting up an imposter program? That is so lame." He glared at Natasha. "All you're doing is slowing everything down. Cutting our productivity in half."

Dylan glanced at Natasha, but she was studying Campbell with a small frown on her face.

"Look, Jerry. Go work on that last bug. I need you to find it."

Campbell cursed under his breath, but he nodded. "Don't worry, Dylan. I will. But you'd better ask your computer expert here how much time she's costing us—and why." He pushed past Dylan and stomped out.

When Dylan turned back to Natasha, she was staring at her computer screen.

"Is he right?"

Natasha sat and manipulated the mouse. Campbell had seen her rerouting code on her monitor. Problem was, she hadn't left the file open. He must have opened it.

"I told you the imposter program would slow the system some," she said. She accessed the log file and checked her computer's sign ons.

"You said it would be imperceptible."

"I said *almost*. Campbell was always a gamble.

He's a really good programmer. As soon as he tried to do something—send an e-mail, check a household file, he'd know. He immediately recognized what I'd done."

"He didn't have but—what—five minutes. Won't the hacker be able to do the same thing?"

She shook her head. "Campbell's intimately familiar with the whole program. Even the best hacker has to know where he is in the program—where to start. Our guy can't afford to leave himself open and unprotected that long."

"Still, doesn't it surprise you that Campbell spotted it in less than fifteen minutes?"

"Not really. He's tied directly into the real server, just like you are, remember. You two will notice a definite difference between the operation of the server that hides the interface and the one that handles e-mail and household computer activities."

"So he must have been accessing one of those areas."

She nodded. "I'm sure he was. My question is, why was he so upset?" She lifted her head and looked across the hall. Campbell was hunched over his computer, typing very fast. "Do you think he could be the inside source?"

"No. I don't think he'd sabotage his own work." Dylan looked less certain than he sounded.

"I hope you're right. But just to be safe, I'm going to check his e-mail history and local files." She took a look at the quarantined files. It was a good thing Campbell hadn't gotten far enough on her computer to spot the suspicious files.

"Here. Ten minutes ago he tried to send an e-mail with an attachment. My quarantine caught it."

"What kind of attachment?" He came around and looked at the screen.

"I'm opening his e-mail in an editing program that will prevent attachments from executing. There—the attached file is computer code."

"From the interface software?"

"It looks like it. Apparently Campbell has sent himself some of the software."

Dylan straightened, then slapped his palm against the door. "Go to bed, Natasha. I'm going to have a word with Campbell."

Natasha watched Dylan disappear through a door and appear on the other side. He stalked straight into the virtual surgery lab and confronted Campbell.

His intensity and magnetism wasn't cooled by two walls of glass. She pressed her palms against her cheeks, trying to cool the heat there. For the first time in her life, she was having trouble concentrating on the job at hand.

Usually she could lose herself in fascination with the computer code. It had a beauty, a symmetry, which for her rivaled a symphony or a compelling painting.

But now, her fascination was fixed on Dylan Stryker. Just being in the same room with him stirred sensations that scared her.

When he'd kissed her in the tunnel-house, her insides had turned to mush. She'd forgotten all about the hacker, the interface program, even the claustrophobic tunnel.

That couldn't happen again. She reminded herself that her goal was to catch the hacker and get out of this suffocating fortress.

She had no business having sexual thoughts about Dylan.

NATASHA WOKE UP already reaching for her weapon. What had she heard? There it was again. Her mobile radio. It crackled with static as she grabbed it.

"Agent Rudolph."

It was Mintz. Natasha's pulse hammered in her temple as she glanced at her watch. Just after 5:00 a.m.

"The west fire door. Now. Don't wake Dylan."

"On my way," she said as she picked up her fanny pack. "Out."

The sirens started by the time she got into her boots and pulled a dark sweater over her head. She drew her weapon as she opened the door to the hall.

Ben's door opened. *Dylan.*

"Get back inside," she whispered.

"What is it?" His sleepy eyes glimmered in the dim night-lights.

"Stay with Ben. Mintz called me."

His gaze sharpened. "I'm going with you."

"Dylan!" She took two steps and grasped a handful of his T-shirt. "Mintz wants you here. Ben is the most important thing!"

His eyes flashed, but with a grimace, he nodded.

She turned and headed for the stairs, descending them slowly, her gun aimed and ready to fire.

The west side fire door was open. She stiffened and slowed her pace.

"Mintz?" she called out.

Storm stuck his head in the door and motioned to her. "Hey, sugar, here we are."

"What's going on?"

Storm guided her through the door and around an area near the door where several large spotlights were aimed. Smoke was rising from the debris, and a distinctive smell filled the air.

Natasha's whole body went numb with dread for an instant. "Do I smell RDX?"

Storm nodded. "Royal Demolition eXplosive. A very small amount. Enough to cause an explosion—not enough to destroy anything. We've got men scouring the perimeter, but we don't believe the RDX was brought in from outside."

Natasha took in the activity around her. Mintz was crouched over the smoking debris, with Hector and Robby standing on either side of him. Robby had a digital camera, and was photographing the entire area.

"How long ago did it go off?"

Storm glanced at his watch. "It's been seven minutes."

"I didn't hear anything."

He shook his head. "We didn't, either. Like I said, it was a small explosion, very contained. We're looking for the trigger now."

She returned her weapon to her fanny pack. "Who heard it?"

"Nobody. Hector was working the front doors. He saw it on one of the camera monitors."

Hector again. "I want to see the disks. We should be able to identify who set it."

"If they're inside, they'll know about the surveillance. They probably hid their face."

She looked back at the door. "Why didn't the explosion trigger lockdown?"

"Too small."

"Damn it." The panic bar. It allowed the door to be opened from the inside without detection. "No footprints, either?"

"Ground's dry. I doubt we'll get much."

Mintz straightened from his crouch and walked over to them. "Nice work, Agent Storm," he said, his face lined with worry. "The trigger was a cell phone. Very simple. A small amount of RDX, hot wires, probably triggered by calling the phone."

"From the outside?" Natasha asked.

"I'd bet a year's salary on it."

"How many men do you have searching the outside perimeter?"

"Eight. But whoever did this is long gone." Mintz wiped a shaky hand over his hair.

Natasha touched his arm. "We'll get them."

He nodded. "Where's Dylan?"

"He's with Ben."

Mintz met her gaze and she knew he was thinking the same thing she was. This was too close. Ben couldn't stay here. Dylan shouldn't stay.

"I'd better let him know."

"Alfred. I'll do it."

He shook his grizzled head. "Nope. It's not your responsibility. I should have insisted weeks ago that he and Ben get out of here. We could have moved the interface then. We can't move it now."

"But Ben can be moved."

He looked up at her, pain etched on his weathered face. He rubbed his chin. "Dylan won't go. Not now."

She nodded, wanting to cry. "I know."

Mintz pressed his lips together and glanced up at the house. "Take over the scene."

"I'm going with you. Storm can handle this."

This time Mintz didn't object. "Dust for prints," he said to Storm. "We've got prints on all the house staff and the security team."

"I'm on it," Storm said.

"As soon as I get back we'll start questioning the staff."

Natasha followed Mintz up the stairs to Ben's room. Mintz tapped softly on the door then turned the knob. Dylan was sitting beside Ben's bed.

He stood, anticipation and dread etched on his face. "Well?"

"Come out here," Mintz said softly.

Dylan glanced down at his sleeping son, then brushed his fingers across Ben's forehead in a gesture so tender it sent an aching pain through Natasha's heart.

She backed up as Dylan stepped into the hall and closed Ben's door.

Mintz gestured toward her room. She went in first and turned on the lights, revealing her unmade bed and the pile clothes she'd shed the night before.

Dylan barely waited until the door closed to turn on Mintz.

"What happened?"

"Dylan—" Natasha started, but Mintz held up his hand.

"There was an explosion."

Dylan's face drained of color. "Explosion? Another one? Why didn't I hear it?"

"It was a small blast, very contained, very deliberate."

"Where? Who was hurt?"

Mintz gripped Dylan's shoulder. "Son, you need to calm down. You're exhausted. You're burning yourself up."

"Stop trying to protect me, Alfred. You're working as hard as I am."

"The explosion was near the west wing fire door. The door was unlocked. There's no evidence that anyone came over the fence."

Natasha stood immobilized by the fear and anguish roiling around her. She hadn't realized how much the two men depended on each other. They were like father and son. The bond between them was palpable.

Dylan glanced at her. She hoped her expression didn't reflect how worried she was—about him, about Ben.

"If they didn't come over the fence—" His eyes

flared like an oxygen flame as the truth penetrated. "Inside?" he croaked. "The explosion was set from the inside?"

Mintz rubbed a hand over his face and nodded. "Using a cell phone. Detonated by a cell phone call that activated the trigger. I've got men canvassing the entire perimeter to verify that not one inch has been compromised. I've given instructions that no one is to leave the grounds until we say so."

"We're going to question all the staff. We'll find out who did this," Natasha said.

"Dylan—"

Dylan held up his hands and shook his head at Alfred. "No. Don't even say it. I am not sending Ben away. He wouldn't understand."

"I'm hoping you'll go with him." Mintz's face was grim.

"You know I can't do that," Dylan rasped. His jaw twitched with tension. "The prototype can't be moved."

"Listen to me, son. I want Ben to walk, too. But your lives are worth more than that contraption. You're going to get him and yourself killed if you don't get him out of here."

Natasha backed toward the door. This was too intimate, too private. She shouldn't be here. This was a family matter. Dylan and Mintz had to work this out together.

It was no place for her.

She turned the knob and slipped out. As she closed the door behind her, she heard Dylan's anguished voice, but she couldn't make out what he said.

For a few seconds she stood there in the dimly lit hallway, her jaw clenched, her eyes stinging, until she finally forced the tears back. She took a long breath and headed back downstairs to help Storm collect evidence.

OH, BOY. This was not good. Natasha stared at the computer screen, her mouth going dry and her heartbeat fluttering in her throat as her eyes skimmed the lines and lines of code.

She'd finished helping Storm with the evidence several hours ago and had spent the afternoon searching for errors in the interface code.

The system had alerted her to a hit on the shell server. She'd signed on immediately and traced back the hit. It had been bold and reckless. The hacker had stayed on the system much longer than was safe. He was careful and very good, but he was also cocky.

Still, he had a right to be. Natasha swallowed against rising panic. *It was Tom.* The best hacker she'd ever seen. In a way, she had to admire him. He'd gotten a lot better in the past eight years.

He'd even tried to change his signature, and he'd done a good job of it. If a hacker was good enough to recognize the patterns that made his code unique, he could deliberately change them, like a felon could burn or file his prints. But nobody could change everything. Some of his signature was still there. It was just harder to detect.

She stretched and looked across the hall to Dylan's virtual surgery lab. It was empty.

She was worried about him. It had been over six hours since she'd left him and Mintz talking. Her heart ached for both of them. She knew—they all knew—what had to be done. But Dylan was so stressed and exhausted. She wasn't sure he'd survive without Ben.

A tiny window popped up at the bottom of her screen. It was notification of an e-mail. Her pulse raced as she opened the message.

Hi Nt FBI eh? Gd luck U need it U won't win this time.

"Damn it," she whispered. Tom knew she was here.

Just then the door to Dylan's lab opened and he entered. He was pale and the lines around his mouth were deeper. He sat at his workstation and picked up the pad and stylus. Then he put them down again and leaned forward, propping his elbows on his knees, and stared at the floor.

His pain reached her through the glass walls, engulfing her. Her whole body ached in sympathy. She had to go to him, give him what little comfort she could offer.

She went through the doors and into his lab.

He didn't even look up.

"Dylan?" she said tentatively.

"Go back to work," he said hoarsely.

"Not right now." She pulled Campbell's chair over and sat beside him. She didn't say anything else, just sat there.

After a couple of minutes of silence, Dylan sat back and wiped his face. A muscle twitched in his jaw.

"Ben's gone." His voice was carefully even.

Pain sliced through her heart and tears stung her eyes. She'd known that Mintz would convince Dylan, but being prepared didn't dull the pain she felt at his anguish.

She wanted to hold him and promise him that everything would be all right. But she knew that wasn't what he needed. She knew he wouldn't believe it. So she stayed quiet.

"Charlene went with him. Alfred arranged for Special Agent Storm to transport them to a safe house." He made a short, sharp sound that could have been a laugh. "Apparently Alfred has been planning this for a while. Obviously, he's got better judgment than I have."

He looked at her for the first time and she saw the haunted determination she'd seen the first time he'd looked at her.

"I don't know what I'll do if anything happens to him."

Natasha took his hand. His fingers tightened around hers. "Nothing's going to happen to Ben," she said. "He's safe. You can stop worrying about him and concentrate on the interface."

He nodded, his eyes on their entwined fingers. He ran his thumb across her knuckles, and then pulled away.

"What are you working on?"

She took a deep breath. She hadn't decided how much to tell him about Tom. "The hacker hit again."

His eyes sparked and he sat up. "Did you stop him?"

She nodded. "Like I told you, he's very good." She paused. She was going to take the coward's way out, at least for now. She told herself that Dylan didn't need the additional stress of knowing that she'd IDed the hacker.

"This was no hit-and-run. This guy's a risk taker. He launched a deliberate attack on the secure area."

"But he didn't get in."

"No. He did linger long enough for me to trace some of his code. I may be able to isolate his signature." She looked at her hands. She wasn't used to lying.

"Explain to me what that means."

"Every hacker has his or her own way of doing things. Every virus or worm or bot he creates contains his code, written in his way. No two people code in exactly the same way, so a hacker's signature can ID him, like a fingerprint."

"Or DNA."

She smiled and shook her head. "Unfortunately not. DNA doesn't change. But a good hacker—no, an *exceptional* hacker can change his signature to a certain extent. He'd have to be savvy enough to recognize his own coding pattern and how it differs from anyone else's."

"And our guy?"

"I'm studying him. I've got my own database of samples from some known hackers."

"So you'll be able to ID him soon?"

Natasha felt queasy. Her hands were shaking. She looked down at them. If she met Dylan's gaze right now, he'd know the truth—she already knew who the hacker was. "Well, I'd better get back to work."

Dylan stood. He touched her cheek and gave her a heartbreaking smile. "Thank you."

She shifted position slightly, just enough to pull away from his fingers. "Just doing my job," she said.

"You've gone far above and beyond. I appreciate it."

Natasha left and went back to her computer, feeling like a traitor. She had no idea what she was going to do about Tom. But she had to come up with something—and fast.

Because she knew that this wasn't just her and her expertise against a malicious hacker. Tom had made that clear in his message. She read it one more time.

Hi Nt FBI eh? Gd luck U need it U won't win this time.

For Tom, it was personal. He wouldn't give up until he'd destroyed her and everyone around her.

She was the reason he was doing this.

Chapter Nine

Natasha stopped in front of the door to the clean room. She hadn't seen Dylan in over twenty-four hours, and she was worried about him.

Mintz had told her he was working in the temperature-controlled, air-filtered room where the prototype device was stored. He was refining the mapping of the nerves and finalizing the corresponding superfine fibers that would take the place of Ben's damaged nerves.

Mintz had also told her not to bother him, yet here she was. Her conscience had been eating at her all day as she studied Tom's code and tried to figure out what his next move would be.

She had to tell Dylan about Tom. He deserved to know just how vengeful the attacks on his home and his computer were. He deserved the choice of keeping her or dismissing her.

She had the sick feeling that if she weren't here,

Tom might have given up after a couple of failed attempts and gone on to an easier target.

She'd already sent an urgent message via Storm to Decker alerting him that Tom was the hacker and that they should assume he was working with a domestic terrorist cell—based on the truck driver's suicide mission.

Now she had to tell Dylan. She knocked on the door, but the flat sound of her knuckles hitting steel told her there was no way anyone inside could hear her. She looked for a buzzer or button, but didn't see anything.

Dylan had told her that she was one of four people who could open any door. Did that include this one? She tried her pass code and fingerprint, and heard the muffled click. She went in, letting the door swing shut behind her with a quiet heavy thud. The sound of forced air surrounded her.

A frisson of alarm slithered down her back. She turned, her breathing suddenly sharp and uneven. The door had a panic bar, like most of the other doors in the house.

Panic bar. Good name. She smiled wryly. Forcing herself to breathe slowly and evenly, she surveyed the room.

It was swathed in shadow. She saw a seating area—a couch and chair on one side. A desk with a computer console was against one wall.

Her eyes were drawn toward a bright area on the opposite wall—a small area curtained by heavy translucent plastic sheeting.

The clean room. Where Dylan and Campbell worked on assembling the interface hardware. It was set up to filter dust and keep the temperature and humidity at a controlled level.

That's where the forced air was coming from. The clean room was positive pressure, which meant that anyone entering would be subjected to a strong downdraft of clean air—it kept out dust and lint.

She scanned the length of the room. It was empty.

"Dylan?" she called as she stepped away from the door. To her left a recess in the wall provided the only other light. A small sign hung next to it. She stepped closer.

Restroom And Showers. Light spilled out from a short, tiled corridor.

"Dylan?" Her voice sounded small and scared.

She heard a noise. She hesitated. Should she go in?

Just then he appeared wearing jeans and nothing else. His face and torso were sprinkled with drops of water and he rubbed a towel over his wet hair.

The sight of him backlit by the shower room's fluorescent glow struck Natasha speechless for a second. His bare arms and shoulders rippled with sleek muscles. His abs were lean and defined. And the sparkling water droplets made him look sprinkled with fairy dust.

Her insides tingled with awareness. Her mouth watered at the remembered the taste of him. Her fingers remembered his skin.

He lowered the towel and stopped, surprised. "Tasha—"

She dragged her eyes away from his abs. "I'm sorry. I was worried—"

"No, no. It's okay." He gave his hair one last swipe with the towel then tossed it behind him. "I was just taking a break while the diagnostic program runs."

His golden skin glimmered. Natasha watched two little drops on his chest merge into one and trickle down toward his belly. She swallowed and blinked, imagining that she felt his heat radiating over her. She didn't think she'd ever get used to the magnetism of his presence.

"How—how's it going?" she stammered, forcing her gaze upward, to meet his.

He shrugged. "I'll know when the diagnostic is finished." He wiped a hand across his face, then pushed his fingers through his wet hair, spiking it. His eyelashes were wet and matted together like star points around his eyes.

He sent her a curious glance. "Did you need something?"

She opened her mouth to tell him about Tom and how she knew him, but she couldn't. In fact she wasn't sure she could speak at all. Not with him standing half-naked in front of her. "I—was just worried about you," she stammered. "I haven't seen you all day."

His mouth turned up. "I'm okay. I'll be better if that diagnostic finishes with no errors." He glanced toward the clean room then looked at his watch. "It's been running over an hour. Campbell started it around ten."

"I saw him in the virtual surgery lab."

"Really? I guess he's trying to make up for what he did."

"You talked to him? What did he say?"

"He said he was just sending files of his code to his home computer."

Natasha raised her brows. "Did he say why?"

Dylan shrugged, sending rivulets of water sliding down his pecs and over his belly.

She forced herself to look at his face.

"He said he was proud of his work. Said none of it could be used to create or destroy the interface."

"You believe him?"

"I have to. But you *are* quarantining his e-mails, right?"

"Right." She quirked her mouth into a smile. "So what about you? How long have you been down here?"

He shook his head and a shadow crossed his face. "Not long enough. The interface isn't finished until the diagnostic runs without error. So far, we've run it eleven times."

"Eleven errors?"

"You know how it goes. Fix one error and another that was hidden by the first pops up."

A beeping sound came from the clean room.

Dylan's head angled. "It's finished." He met her gaze, fear and hope shining in his eyes.

She nodded and tried to smile. Hope and need radiated from him, hot as a desert wind. She didn't know what he'd do if the program was still buggy.

He crossed the room to the computer workstation, studied the monitor for a moment, then reached across the desk to the printer. He retrieved the pages and shuffled them.

Natasha walked slowly over to stand beside him. She didn't say anything, just watched him intently. Her body was tense with dread and anticipation.

He studied the printout, then looked back at the monitor. He typed something, clicked with the mouse, and stared at the screen.

She waited, holding her breath.

When he finally raised his gaze to hers, he looked stunned.

Her heart seized in her chest. *Oh, no.* Had the program erred out? She couldn't speak. All she could do was touch his forearm in silent support.

Slowly his eyes changed, and his stunned expression morphed into disbelief, then hope.

"Dylan?" Natasha whispered, almost soundlessly.

"It's—" he stopped and cleared his throat "—it's finished."

She heard his words, but for an instant they didn't make any sense. "Finished?"

His face transformed. He shook his head in wonder. The bulging tension in his jaw and neck faded, and he grinned. "It works! The interface works!" He laughed. "The diagnostic finished with no errors!"

Natasha's throat clogged with emotion.

He gripped her upper arms, his face beaming. "No errors. Do you know what that means?"

She smiled. "You can operate! You can make him walk!"

He wrapped his arms around her, hugging her tightly. She hugged him back. His hard bare torso against hers was as hot and silky smooth as she'd imagined it.

His shoulders quivered and his breath hitched.

She caressed his hair and neck. After a few seconds he bent his head and buried his face against her neck. She felt his hot tears.

She was crying, too, her tears mixing with the water droplets on his skin. She was so happy for them. Ben could be freed from the prison of his leg braces, and Dylan could finally shed the guilt that weighed him down. He could help his son.

She took a deep breath, breathing in his familiar scent. She cried with happiness—for him, for Ben.

But after several seconds, she could no longer maintain a remote happiness for his success.

Her insides vibrated with sensation, her thighs tightened in anticipation. She was mortified that she was turned on by him right now, when he'd just found out that he could make his child walk again.

"Thank you," he muttered hoarsely against her neck as he tightened his embrace.

"You did it. You finished the interface." She should pull away. She shouldn't be enjoying the strength and safety of his embrace. Every inch of his skin that touched hers shouldn't burn her with erotic fire. His muscular thighs shouldn't be taunting hers. His hard chest shouldn't be rubbing so sensually against her breasts, tightening their tips as his uneven breaths stoked the fire of her passion. And she shouldn't want to slide her palms over his pecs to feel his crisp, sparse chest hair.

She tried to keep her breathing even, tried to pull away, but her body refused to cooperate. The pull of his burning intensity was unbearably erotic.

His arms relaxed a bit and he took a small step backward. "Natasha? Are you all right?"

Thank goodness one of them was strong.

She sighed in relief and lowered her arms. "Sure." Her voice broke. "I'm just so happy for you and Ben."

At the mention of his son's name his gaze darkened. He nodded. "I need to call NSA. Set up an operating room. The clock is ticking."

"It's late. Why don't you sleep, then call them tomorrow." She laid her palm against his chest.

He caught her hand in his and kissed her palm. "I couldn't have done this without you."

"What little I did," she said, "was my pleasure." She smiled at him and gently pulled away.

But he didn't let go. Instead, his embrace subtly changed. It was no longer a hug—it was a caress. His muscles relaxed, turned sinuous and supple. Her body felt the change in his, and it fed her growing desire.

His hands slid down her back, gentle and caressing. They spanned her waist, then moved lower, to her hips. He urged her against him with gentle pressure and small adjustments of his stance, until she was caught, one leg between his, with his pulsing erection pressed against her in undisguised need. She closed her eyes. She should stop him, but she didn't.

He bent his head just enough to reach her mouth. As his lips brushed hers she gasped. He groaned and his body grew harder and hotter.

"Tasha?" he whispered, as if asking for her permission.

She should say no. Stop. *Something.* But her vocal cords were paralyzed, and her brain was fixated on one thing—his hot strong body undulating against hers. His erection was rigid, straining against her belly as his lips skimmed across her skin.

She lifted her head enough to kiss him back. As his kiss stirred her, she could no longer deny to him or herself how much she wanted him. Ever since their kiss in the tunnel-house, she'd craved his soap and cinnamon scent, his hard, sinewy body, his firm, mobile mouth.

He plunged his fingers into her hair as his tongue urged her lips to part. She responded. He tasted like coffee. He felt like silk-covered steel.

Her hands ran greedily over his pecs, his muscled abdomen and around to stroke the bare flesh of his back. She traced his ridged spine and caressed the lean muscles that rippled under her touch.

He engulfed her in sensation. His hands slipped beneath her sleeveless top. He traced each rib, moving up, up, until his thumbs grazed the underside of her breasts.

She shivered with reaction. Her breasts tightened and a liquid yearning pooled between her thighs.

"Tasha? Are you okay?" he whispered against her ear.

"I don't know," she murmured, arching her neck as he trailed kisses along her skin, finding erogenous zones she never knew she had. "Yes."

Dylan groaned under his breath as his body responded immediately, painfully to her supple strength. He ran his mouth and tongue along her neck, her jaw, the underside of her chin. She tasted the way he'd known she would. Like springtime and strawberries.

He returned to her mouth, kissing her slowly and thoroughly, pulling her even closer until he felt fused to her by their heat.

His erection pulsed with desperate desire. His breathing turned ragged. He was too close to the edge. He'd never be able to hold out. But as much as he wanted to overpower her and propel them both to climax, he held back.

Natasha had always seemed so strong, but right now she felt fragile, breakable in his arms. She raised her gaze to his and the longing and trust in her green eyes scared him.

She flattened her hands against his chest. Her palms were hot. Her fingers curled into his chest hair as he teased her mouth and tongue.

He felt the change in her. She relaxed, and his concern that she might break dissipated as her body moved against him with supple grace and strength.

She opened herself to him, offering him her lush, sexy lips, and her perfect, firm body. He took them, feasting on her mouth, caressing her breast until he felt its tip tighten and strain with response.

She opened her eyes, their green depths dark with desire, and looked at him. Then she lowered her head and kissed his chest as her fingers sought and teased his nipples.

Shuddering, clenching his jaw to control his raging hunger, he took her hands and urged her gently toward the sofa. Her gaze flickered, questioning, but she didn't resist when he tenderly lowered her to the cushions.

She shivered.

"Cold?" he asked.

She shook her head. "Nervous."

He smiled at her and slid his arm under her head as he lay beside her. He kissed her eyelids and cheek while he teased her breasts under the thin cotton of her blouse.

Each time he touched a taut, hardened little peak, she moaned quietly. Finally, he bent his head and took an erect nipple in his mouth as he ran his hand down her belly to the button of her jeans.

It was an incredible turn-on to nip and suck at her nipple through the cotton, while her belly rose and fell with her excited breaths.

His arousal grew, throbbed until telltale dampness told him he was dangerously close to losing control.

He pulled back.

Natasha opened her eyes. "Dylan?" she whispered. "Did I—"

He shook his head, trying to control his uneven breathing. "You didn't do anything," he said breathlessly, "except turn me on so completely that I'm about to come."

She gave him a shaky smile, her eyes dewy with desire, her mouth open slightly.

He concentrated on undressing her and himself, hoping the distraction of peeling off two pair of tight jeans would slow him down. He pushed her blouse up and off, and removed first his jeans, then hers.

The sight of her slim naked body sent him dangerously near the edge. His erection pulsed. So much for slowing down. Her body was beautiful. Slender, strong, yet undeniably feminine, with curves in all the right places.

He leaned up on one elbow. "You are so perfect, so beautiful," he whispered. Carefully, reverently, he trailed his fingers down her stomach, enjoying the way her muscles fluttered beneath his touch. He ventured farther, skimming the narrow patch of pale hair to caress her inner thighs. Teasing, tantalizing her until she clutched his wrist.

"Dylan…" she begged breathlessly. "Please." She couldn't stand his teasing another second. She craved his heat, craved his touch. She had to feel him inside her.

"Not yet, Tasha." Dylan kissed her with the same intensity he applied to everything he did. She felt like a stick in a flowing river. Time felt endless, flowing, yet at the same time rushed. She knew, like the stick, that she was about to be shattered, but there was nothing she could do to stop it. Nor did she want to.

Dylan flattened his palm against her belly. Natasha arched against his hand, anticipating what was to come, and he groaned quietly.

"Be still," he whispered. "Don't go so fast."

"I can't—"

His fingers moved lower, to caress her intimately. She knew she was ready for him, but he was relentless. Stroking, teasing, again and again he brought her to the brink of release, only to stop and start it all over again.

He bent and kissed her ribs, the tiny hollow between her breasts, then he trailed his tongue from her midriff to her belly and over the slight swell of her hip bones. All the time his fingers fondled and teased her most sensitive area. She gasped and closed her fingers around his wrist, but she didn't really want him to stop.

He pushed her hand away, then bent farther, replacing his fingers with his mouth, and drove her nearly insane with the feel of his lips and tongue.

She was mad with passion by the time he lifted himself above her.

She gazed into his eyes as she ran her hands down his chest, over his ribs and his taut muscled abdomen.

His fiery blue gaze burned her. His intensity engulfed her. His gentle desperation mirrored her own.

She clutched his buttocks and urged him to finish the seduction he'd started.

Dylan gasped as he entered her. She was tight and hot and ready for him. As he buried himself in her she opened beneath him, accepting him fully, rising to meet him.

The feel of her surrounding him was too much to bear. He fought the overwhelming urge to move, to feel the delicious friction of her tightness.

His urgency warred with his determination to coax her into a slow, endless orgasm.

Beneath him, she shifted and took him more deeply.

He sucked in a sharp breath. "You win," he whispered. He couldn't keep it slow.

She followed his movements, synchronizing perfectly with him, as if they'd always been lovers.

Immediately, her body began to soar toward climax. He could tell by the change in her breathing, by the alteration in the tone of the small sounds she made.

"Look at me," he muttered hoarsely, lifting himself on his arms so he could see her breasts with their puckered nipples rise and fall as he stroked within her.

Her eyes were closed and her mouth was open. She moved in perfect rhythm, taunting him, taking him in, building the passion to a fever pitch.

"Tasha, look at me," he demanded, not sure how long he could last. But he wanted them to feel each other, to reach the ultimate peak together. So he clenched his jaw and waited for her to open her green eyes.

She looked at him. He thrust more quickly, more deeply, and her wide green eyes glazed over. She threw her head back and cried out his name.

Her cry destroyed the last of his control. His body spasmed and his entire being convulsed in a climax so intense he thought he might pass out.

"Tasha," he grated through clenched teeth as he poured into her all the pent-up passion of three years alone.

She wrapped her arms around his neck and kissed him as the pulsing of their bodies slowed. He tasted salty tears, but he didn't even wonder whether they were hers or his own.

He closed his eyes and drifted off to sleep.

"NATASHA, WAKE UP!"

Natasha's eyes flew open and she reached under the pillow for her gun. No gun. No pillow. She blinked.

"Here. Here are your clothes."

Dylan was standing over her, holding out her jeans and top. The room was dimly lit and the sound of an ink-jet printer echoed loudly.

Suddenly, she realized she was naked. The only thing covering her was a thin blanket. She sat up, pulling the blanket with her.

Frowning, Dylan dropped her clothes beside her on the couch and turned away. By the time she'd dressed, he was collecting pages from the printer.

The interface. She glanced at her watch. Seven o'clock in the morning. They'd slept all night. If she knew Dylan, he was furious that he'd wasted eight hours. And furious with her for distracting him.

She watched him. He'd put on a T-shirt with his jeans, and his stern expression made him look like the intense genius he was, rather than the tender lover she'd known briefly last night.

Last night. She shivered as small aftershocks of her climax rippled through her. Her experience was relatively limited, but she knew with an unshakable certainty that what had happened between them was special.

A sudden panic surged through her as she studied Dylan's face. Her first thought—that he'd be angry with her, was right on the money. But that was okay. He had every right to blame her for the time they'd wasted. She knew NSA would have waited until this morning to transport the device, but Dylan didn't.

She pushed her fingers through her hair and started toward him.

Her movement caught his eye. He looked up from under his brows. "Get out of here. I don't want anyone walking in on us. I'm sure Alfred has already figured out where we are, but the rest of the staff doesn't need to know."

His voice was even, but though she'd expected them, his words hurt. "Dylan, I know you're—"

"Don't say anything. I apologize. We were both exhausted. Our defenses were down. Leave it at that."

"Our defenses were down?" She gaped at him as doubt began to erode her confidence. Anger was one thing. But his cold arrogant analysis of the intimacy they'd shared frightened her. She'd given him everything. Now he was rejecting it. Rejecting her. Turning what happened into a mistake.

He nodded and turned his attention back to the printouts. "I've got to review these, make sure I'm right. Then I need to get the device packed for transport. There's a lot to do if I'm going to operate on Ben tomorrow."

Natasha stood there for a moment as she tried to reconcile the coldly determined scientist with the tender lover who had held her and loved her the night before, or the desperate loving father who would do anything to save his son's legs.

As pain arrowed through her, she told herself again that she couldn't blame him. He was trying to save his son.

She turned toward the door just as a click and

a faint sound of metal sliding against metal told her someone was coming in. The door swung open.

It was Mintz.

Natasha breathed a sigh of relief. Thank goodness. Alfred might disapprove, but he was discreet.

He barely acknowledged her as he strode up to Dylan, his face ominously grim.

Dylan looked up, his face shining like an angel's. "Alfred! The interface is finished. We need to get in touch with NSA. I'm ready to operate on Ben's legs."

"Dylan—"

Natasha heard the dire tone in Mintz's voice. It spooked her.

She moved closer to Dylan, following an instinctive urge to shield him.

There was something wrong—terribly wrong. Mintz was more upset than she'd ever seen him.

Dylan frowned at him for an instant, then his frown turned into a mask of abject fear. "Alfred, what's wrong?"

Mintz wiped a shaky hand down his face.

Natasha froze, her heart catapulting into her throat. *No. Not Ben.*

"Son, something has happened."

Chapter Ten

"Something—? What? It's not Ben, is it?" Dylan's voice rasped. His face was pale as he held out his hands in a defensive gesture. "No, Alfred. Don't—"

Natasha met Mintz's gaze. He nodded. She moved closer to Dylan's side.

"Alfred, tell me!"

"Ben and Charlene got to the safe house by five yesterday. A short while ago, their guard was shot and they were removed from the house."

"Removed—?" Dylan laughed, a short sharp sound with no amusement in it. "Where is he?"

"Son—"

"No! He was supposed to be *safe* there. You said he would be. Where—is—my—son?" His voice was broken. His blue eyes were dull. He was disintegrating right in front of them.

Natasha reached for his hand but he pulled

away, still warding them off. Doing his best to ward off the truth.

"I've got to find him. Alfred, we've got to find him." His face distorted with grief. "Dear God, what will I do?"

Mintz gripped his shoulder. "Dylan, you've got to calm down. The FBI is already on it. They'll find him."

Dylan could barely think. His entire body was on fire with fear for Ben's safety. His chest cramped, cutting off his breath. Alfred's words echoed at the edge of his mind.

FBI. He glared at his friend. "FBI? Are you kidding me? The FBI hasn't done anything, but make things worse." He included Natasha in his glare.

"What did they do when my wife was killed? Nothing." He swiped at his stinging eyes. "Everybody keeps telling me everything's going to be fine. But that's not true, is it? Nothing is fine." He took a shuddering breath.

"You two got what you wanted. You took Ben away from me—for his *safety.*" He swallowed against the huge lump in his throat. "Now he's in danger. He was safe *here!*"

"Dylan," Natasha said. "I promise you they'll find him."

"*You!* You can't promise me anything. You

don't know." He rubbed the back of his neck. "You can't even figure out who the hacker is." He stopped, his hand on his neck.

The hacker. Of course. "Can you send him a message?" He frowned at Natasha.

She narrowed her eyes. "The hacker? I could, but why? You're not seriously thinking of—"

"Send him message. Tell him I'll give him everything if he ets my son go unharmed."

"You can't do that."

He sent her a withering glance. "I can and I will. The hacker took him. Didn't he?"

He intercepted the glance Natasha sent toward Alfred. "Both of you know it's the hacker. Do it."

"Dylan, you can't negotiate with terrorists. It's suicide. They'll take everything you'll give them, but there's no guarantee they'll let Ben go."

"He's three years old. He can't identify them. He's of no use to them after they get the interface program."

"Exactly. Dylan, he's of *no use*. This is a ruthless, greedy man who doesn't care about anyone except himself. He'll never let Ben go."

He met her gaze, suspicion tightening his chest. "He? You know who he is?"

Her eyes widened. "I—I can't be positive."

Dylan glared at her. "You know. Who is he? Are

you protecting him?" He reached for her arm, but she whirled out of his reach.

"All right, both of you—that's enough." Alfred stepped between him and Natasha, gripping Dylan's shoulders.

"Agent Rudolph, your fellow agents have been pulled to join the search for Ben." Alfred held Dylan's gaze as he spoke. "And Special Agent Decker asked me to have you contact him."

"Yes, sir." She turned on her heel and left the room.

Dylan watched her go. He could hardly think, he was so numb with shock and fear. "She's protecting the hacker."

Alfred shook him once. "She's not. And when you start thinking rationally you'll know she's not."

Dylan squeezed his eyes shut. His throat burned, his chest ached. His pulse thrummed in his temples. "I've lost him, haven't I? I sent him away. I betrayed my little boy."

Alfred shook his head. "No you didn't."

"Yes." He looked into his friend's eyes. "Do you know what I did? I spent the night with her. I indulged myself like a horny kid. Know what I was doing when my child was stolen? I was sleeping."

"Dylan, listen to me. I want you to snap out of this." Alfred released his grip. "I'm glad you finally got some sleep, no matter how you managed it."

"You're glad?"

"That's right. You weren't going to last another day without collapsing. At least now you're rested." Alfred glanced beyond Dylan's shoulder toward the clean room. "Did you say the device is finished?"

Dylan nodded miserably.

"Good. Let's get it packed and transported to a secure facility. Then it will be ready and waiting when we get Ben back."

Alfred's husky voice penetrated Dylan's grief and guilt. He was right. Dylan couldn't afford to break down, couldn't afford the luxury of wallowing in guilt. He had to be ready.

He straightened and met Alfred's gaze. "Call NSA. It's ready to go. I just need to get it packed into the special transport box."

Alfred nodded. "I'll send Campbell down to help." Then he quickly and awkwardly hugged Dylan and gave him a pat on the back.

Dylan's eyes stung and his throat clogged up. "Alfred," he croaked as the older man turned to leave. "Thanks."

NATASHA WALKED OUTSIDE to the play area and called Decker, but his information on the abductors was sketchy. The guard had been a Deputy

U.S. Marshall. He'd been pronounced dead on arrival at the hospital.

She asked about Storm and Gambrini, and found out they were helping to secure the crime scene and canvass for possible witnesses.

As she disconnected, Mintz appeared from the kitchen.

"How's Dylan?" she asked.

He rubbed a hand over his jaw. "Not good. I got him to prepare the interface for transport."

Natasha nodded. "At least that'll keep him occupied for a while."

"I told him he needed to be ready to operate as soon as Ben is found."

She studied the ex-military man as guilt bored a hole in her heart. "Mintz—I need to tell you what happened."

"I know what happened."

"He told you?"

He nodded. "Not really, but it wasn't too hard to figure out."

Her cheeks burned. "I didn't mean it to happen—"

Mintz held up a hand. "You don't have to explain. I'm just glad he got some sleep. Did you find out anything from your boss?"

"No. Just that the guard was a deputy marshal. He was DOA."

"So there's no intel on Ben and Charlene's whereabouts?"

"Nothing."

Mintz stared out beyond the overgrown hedge to the open field beyond.

Natasha watched him, knowing what was coming. She swallowed, wishing she'd done what she'd intended to do last night—told Dylan about Tom.

"Do you think this is the hacker's doing?"

Natasha moistened her dry lips. "Yes."

Mintz faced her. "And you know who he is."

It took all her courage not to look away. "Yes."

Mintz nodded. He crossed his arms, and she knew she wasn't going anywhere until she explained.

"His name is Tom. I met him when—"

"Why don't you wait and tell Dylan."

"Alfred—I wasn't sure until last night."

"Come on. Let's go down to the lab."

She followed Mintz downstairs and into the virtual surgery lab, where Dylan was placing a tiny, bubble-wrapped package into a small metal box that was sitting on the desk. The box had four suspension arms attached to the inside. The tiny package would float on the suspension arms.

"Is it ready?" Mintz asked.

Dylan nodded. "Just as soon as Campbell burns the program off onto DVD." He closed the box and locked it. "All we need to do is let NSA know to come and get it. Meanwhile I need to put it back into the clean room. The temperature is controlled in there, and dust and detritus are at a minimum."

Campbell retrieved a disk from his computer. "Here we go. Two copies. I'll take them to the clean room with the transport box." He set the disks on top of the metal case and headed out of the room and down the hall.

Dylan turned to Mintz. "What is it? Have you heard something?"

Mintz looked at Natasha.

She ignored the ache in her heart and did her best to stay composed. "Dylan, I know the hacker."

"You do?" His eyes lit up. "Have you told your boss? Are they going to pick him up?"

She held out her hands, palms up. "Wait. I don't just know who he is, I *know* him."

"You know—" Dylan's face registered shock. "You didn't just figure that out this morning," he said accusingly. His blue eyes flared like an oxygen-fed flame.

"No." She steeled herself against his anger. "Last night."

"Last night? You knew when—" He stopped, his fists clenched, his face a distorted mask of anger and pain. "Why didn't you tell me?" He bit off each word.

Mintz took two steps, inserting himself between them.

She shook her head miserably. "I should have, I know." She couldn't bring herself to look into his angry hurt eyes. "I wasn't a hundred percent sure until I read the e-mail he sent."

"E-mail. The man who stole my son sent you an e-mail and you didn't think it was worth mentioning?"

Natasha looked from Dylan to Mintz. Both of them were glaring at her. "I notified my boss. Tom's too smart to leave a clear trail. Decker will start a search, but I'm afraid the only way we're going to be able to trace him is through his hacking attempts."

She took a shaky breath and blinked against the stinging in her eyes. "I went to the clean room to tell you."

Dylan's blue eyes flashed with fire as he looked at her in disgust. "And what? It slipped your mind?"

His harsh words hurt. He'd been there, too. *He* had distracted her, but she knew it was her fault. She could have stopped him and she didn't. She'd wanted him as much as he had her.

She dropped her gaze. And now it was too late. There was nothing she could say or do to fix this. She'd endangered Ben because she hadn't wanted to admit that she'd once been a hacker, like Tom.

Dylan rubbed his temple. "So, Agent Rudolph. Do you and *Tom* keep in touch?"

"No! Of course not. I haven't seen him in eight years. He tried to frame me for hacking into the FBI's domestic terrorist database."

"I think you need to leave." In a split second, Dylan's white-hot anger changed to icy calm.

His words flayed open her heart as cleanly and efficiently as a scalpel. Her stomach felt queasy, and a huge lump lodged in her throat.

"Hold on, son," Mintz said. "Don't go off half-cocked. We need her. No sense letting your personal feelings get in the way of saving Ben."

"My personal feelings? It can't *get* more personal. My son is missing. The person who's supposed to be stopping the hacker turns out to be best buddies with him."

Natasha swallowed, and resisted the urge to wipe her burning eyes. "Sir, I'll be happy to call my boss and request a replacement—or you can. But please understand. Eight years ago, Tom was the best. But he was greedy and psychopathically unconcerned about anyone but himself. He's a classic narcissist. From what I've seen him do these past few days, he's still the best." She shrugged. "Or close."

Dylan's eyes narrowed as he studied her. "You think you can beat him."

Did she? Yesterday, she'd have said she didn't know. But today—today a little boy's survival and a father's sanity rested on her shoulders. She had no choice. She *had* to be the best.

"Yes," she said. "I do."

Dylan turned to Mintz. Natasha saw the question in his gaze, and then the softening of his features as Mintz inclined his head a fraction.

"Okay," Dylan said grudgingly. "As long as Alfred believes you. Obviously I can't be objective right now." His voice nearly broke. "Find him. Find him and stop him."

Natasha heard what he didn't say. He hated *her* too much to be objective. She stiffened her back. "I intend to."

"Son, you need to get some rest."

"Rest?" A burst of grim laughter accompanied the word. "I can't rest. My child is out there with strangers. In danger. He thinks I've abandoned him. How can I sleep?"

"Because as soon as we get Ben back, you need to be ready to operate on him." Mintz's face was lined with worry. "You need steady hands and a clear head if you're going to save Ben's legs."

Dylan rubbed his eyes and nodded. "Yeah. Okay." He looked up at Mintz. "You'll let me know as soon as you hear anything?"

The older man squeezed Dylan's shoulder. "The very second."

"Thanks."

Mintz gestured to Natasha. "Agent Rudolph and I are going upstairs to contact the FBI. We'll see—"

A muffled explosion hit Natasha's ears. A split second later, the sirens whooped in a long-short-short cadence.

"That's Ben's play area." Mintz jerked his mobile radio from its belt clip.

Natasha's hand went to her fanny pack, feeling the reassuring weight of her Glock.

"Come with me, Natasha," Mintz commanded. "You—" he pointed to Dylan "—stay here."

Dylan knew that the explosion had to be massive to be heard in the basement. He glared at Alfred. "Hell, no! I'm going with you."

Alfred opened his mouth to argue, but Dylan lifted his chin. Alfred clamped his jaw.

He followed Alfred and Natasha up the back stairs and through the family quarters. As they ran, Alfred yelled into the radio.

"What's going on?"

Static crackled and Dylan couldn't make out the answer.

"What did they say?" he puffed.

"Robby's on the front door. He said the explosion was deafening up here. It knocked the lights out. We're on generator power."

When Natasha jerked opened the door to the atrium, smoke billowed in.

"What the—" Alfred pulled her back inside. "You two wait here. I'm going to check out the damage."

"I'm going with you." Dylan grabbed his arm.

"Stay here!" Alfred's voice thundered in Dylan's ears, loud enough to overpower the sirens.

He nodded and took a step back. He knew that tone—it was Alfred's Marine Sergeant voice. It wasn't smart to disobey him when he was in military mode.

But Dylan couldn't wait here, doing nothing. His heart thudded painfully against his chest and echoed in his ears. Too much was happening. He felt out of control, helpless. His child was missing, his home was under attack.

Alfred plunged into the smoke. Dylan held on to the door for a few seconds.

Through the haze of smoke he saw two security guards brandishing weapons. They had on masks. One unhooked a spare mask from his belt and tossed it to Alfred.

Natasha pushed the door shut. He turned and glared at her. "I heard what Mintz said," he said shortly.

"You need to let him do his job. Don't make it more difficult."

He didn't answer her. "What do you think happened?"

"I think there's been another attack."

Just then the sirens stopped. "Thank goodness," he breathed. "Those things can drive you insane."

Natasha smiled grimly. "Yes, they can."

Dylan took a good look at her. She looked the way she had the night the truck rammed into his front gates. Competent. Self-assured. She was in her element. She clutched her Glock and stood on the balls of her feet—perfectly balanced, ready for anything. Her hair was twisted up into a ponytail, her top and jeans fit her body snugly— no loose fabric to get in her way if she had to run or fight.

She glanced at him out of the corner of her eye. For an instant their gazes held and his body grew hard at the sight of her. She was gorgeous. There was no part of her that wasn't strong and smooth and feminine. He knew firsthand. And God help him, he hated her for affecting him that way.

She let her gaze travel down and back up his length, and he realized as much as she might fight it, she was just as attracted to him as he was to her.

Alfred pushed the door open, letting in black smoke. Both of them scrambled backward, out of the way as he entered. Alfred bent over in a coughing fit. As the door closed he dug a handkerchief from his pocket and wiped his eyes.

Dylan put an arm around his shoulders. "Are you all right?"

Alfred nodded. His face was wet with sweat and streaked with soot. He swiped the handkerchief across his cheeks and forehead.

"What caused the explosion?" Natasha asked.

Alfred coughed again, and wiped his eyes. "A helicopter."

"A helicopter?" Dylan repeated, trying to make sense of Alfred's words. "It crashed?"

Alfred nodded. "Right into the play area. The kitchen and dining room are destroyed. My men are pumping water in from the reservoir tank, but it's going to take a while to get the temperature down."

"What about injuries?"

Alfred rubbed his chin. "We lost a guard. He was a good man. Been here nearly a year. I never got to know him very well, but Robby liked him." He sighed. "Two men are on their way to the hospital with burns and smoke inhalation."

"I should notify Decker," Natasha said.

"Right, but first I want you two downstairs. Find Campbell and take him with you. I'm initiating terminal lockdown."

"Alfred, you can't."

Alfred leveled a gaze at Dylan. "Yes, I can, and I am."

Dylan glanced at Natasha, who looked as surprised and dismayed as he felt. Her face had turned pale, and she was frowning at Alfred.

"Sir? Are you sure?" she asked.

"The helicopter crash was no accident. It's another suicide mission."

Dylan grimaced. Another man had died trying to hurt him. "But why? All they'd have to do is contact me. I'd give them everything if they'd give me my son."

Alfred shook his head. "I don't know. I suppose it's possible we're dealing with two different attackers."

"That's not likely," Natasha commented.

"I know, but what other explanation is there?"

"Maybe this plan was put into action before we sent Ben to the safe house." She looked from Alfred to Dylan.

Alfred nodded. "Could be. Do you think your hacker knows Ben's no longer here?"

"Depends on who his informant is."

Alfred straightened and cleared his throat. "You two get down to the basement now! Thank goodness Cook is off today. If she'd been in the kitchen, she'd have been killed. I'm keeping the guards on duty until the fires are out and the house is safe. Robby will report to the locals that this was an accident. He'll let them in to process the scene and recover the body of the pilot."

Terminal lockdown meant cutting off all means of entry to the basement from the house. "I'm not going down there and leave you alone up here," Dylan told the older man.

Alfred's jaw worked as he folded his handkerchief in half and half again. "I'll be down there before I initiate lockdown. I plan to be with you, to protect you."

"I'm more worried about *your* safety."

"I know." Alfred's dark eyes softened for an instant before he turned back into Marine Sergeant Mintz. "Now get downstairs so I can concentrate on getting the house ready."

IN THE BASEMENT, Natasha headed straight for her computer. She needed to screen and transfer files from the imposter server. If Tom sent another e-mail, she didn't want him to see an unusual delay in response. They couldn't afford to give him a reason to suspect an imposter program. It wouldn't take him long to realize that his e-mails were being diverted.

Dylan followed her and leaned against the door frame. "What are you doing?"

She squeezed her eyes shut for an instant. "I'm

keeping the system secure. If I don't screen e-mails every hour or so, the sender could run a diagnostic and figure out that the e-mail and household accounts are on separate servers."

"The sender. Tom." He crossed his arms.

Natasha looked up and met his hot gaze. "I am so sorry," she whispered.

His jaw clenched as he stood silent for a few beats. "Why didn't you tell me?" he asked quietly.

"I tried. That's why I came to the clean room. But you were so excited about finishing the interface, and then—"

He stood there, dark and dangerously handsome, waiting for her to finish her sentence. "And then?"

"You were right," she said miserably. "I got distracted."

His gaze sharpened, bright as the sun's reflection on polished steel. He pressed his crossed arms closer to his chest, making his biceps ripple.

"Yeah," he said finally, tearing his gaze away from her and studying the toe of his shoe. "Me, too."

She stared at him in surprise. He'd actually said it. She'd have figured he'd blame her for seducing him. But here he was, standing in front of her, admitting that making love with her had affected him, too.

"I wanted to lash out at you. I wanted everything that had happened to be your fault. But the truth is, it's mine."

"Your fault? How?"

He rubbed his cheek and chin. "I was daydreaming about you instead of working on Ben's interface."

She swallowed the flutter at the back of her throat. "But you finished it!"

"And Ben is gone."

His anguish hit her, white-hot. "You can't blame yourself for that. That's not your fault. You couldn't have foreseen what happened."

"I should have kept him here. He'd have been safe here."

"Dylan, the helicopter crashed into his play area. What if he'd been out there?"

His eyes registered shock and a pained sound escaped his lips. He crossed his arms again. "He's never spent a night without me. He's got to be terrified," he said hoarsely, pain visible in his eyes.

She stood. "He's got Charlene," she said quietly.

He stared at the floor and shook his head. "We don't know that."

"She was taken, too. She's there with him. I know it. I'm sure Tom doesn't want to be bothered with a child. They'll keep her to take care of him."

"Dear God, I hope you're right." He uncrossed his arms and rubbed his eyes.

Natasha moved closer. She slipped her arms around his waist. "I am right," she whispered as she pulled him closer.

After a brief hesitation, he hugged her, bending to press his cheek against hers. He sighed shakily.

She'd been afraid he'd rebuff her effort at comfort. But he clung to her like a drowning man to a life preserver. His breath warmed her neck and his lean strong arms encircled her, making her feel safe and loved—at least for one moment.

She hoped she could provide the same for him. She turned her head slightly, so her lips barely grazed his cheek.

The sound of a door opening startled them both. He let go of her so fast she nearly overbalanced.

It was Campbell, coming from the direction of the clean room.

She watched Dylan compose his features before turning. "Campbell. Where've you been?"

Campbell looked from one of them to the other, his eyes narrowed in suspicion. "What's going on?" he asked.

"There's been a helicopter crash. We're locking down."

"Helicopter?" Campbell looked confused and alarmed. "What do you mean, *crash?*"

"Just what I said. A helicopter came down right in Ben's play area. Destroyed that part of the house." Dylan's unrelenting gaze pinned Campbell.

Did he suspect his computer expert of being the inside source? Natasha had considered him but she'd had to admit to herself that the only reason he seemed more suspicious than Charlene or Hector or Robby or one of the other guards was because he had access to the interface program.

Truth was, she didn't have any evidence against anyone. As far as her feelings—she didn't trust Hector, but Robby seemed like a stand-up guy. She had trouble believing that Charlene was smart enough or brave enough to do the things the traitor had done, but she couldn't dismiss her. Campbell was probably the most likely candidate. Her problem was that she didn't know all the security guards or the house staff. The traitor might be someone she hadn't even met.

Campbell glanced around. "You're going to lock down the lab?" His brown eyes registered panic. "I can't stay down here."

"You're going to have to."

"How long?" He was practically turning green. Natasha knew how he felt. But he'd been here for two years. He should have gotten used to working in the underground lab.

Dylan shook his head. "I don't know. That's up to Alfred."

"Where's he?"

"Taking care of the final details upstairs."

"I've got to go up there. I need to call my mother."

"You can call her from here."

Campbell's eyes showed white all the way around. "I'm going upstairs."

Dylan laid a hand on Campbell's arm. "You're staying here," he bit out.

Campbell's eyelids fluttered and his throat worked as he met Dylan's fiery blue gaze. Sweat gathered at his hairline. He shook his head but Dylan's grip tightened. So he gave up.

"Okay," he said shakily. "I hope you have some tranqs, Doc."

Dylan let go of him. "I've got a few if you decide you can't live without one."

"Good." Sweat rolled over Campbell's forehead. He swiped a forearm across his face. "Is it hot in here?"

Dylan glanced at Natasha. She thought she saw a glimmer of amusement when he caught her eye. She suppressed a smile. At least she wasn't as bad as Campbell, although she had a niggling suspicion that the bioengineer might be covering the real reason for his worry.

Had he sabotaged the lab? Was he panicking because he was afraid he'd get caught by whatever trap he'd set?

Mintz's footsteps echoed from the back stairwell.

"You know where the water is. Why don't you get a bottle," Dylan said to Campbell.

He shook his head. "I want to hear what Mintz says."

So did Natasha. She wasn't quite sure what locking them in the underground lab would accomplish. It would protect them from an outside attack, but Natasha was more afraid of an assault on their computer programs, especially Dylan's encrypted interface program.

Mintz walked down the hall, straight for the briefing room that adjoined the virtual surgery lab. He used his fingerprint and pass code to open a metal box hanging on the wall. As Natasha watched, he pulled levers and dialed in codes.

A metallic click echoed through the lab. *Lockdown.* They were locked in, twelve feet underground. A trickle of sweat ran down her back. Now she was starting to act like Campbell.

Mintz motioned to them through the glass walls.

"I'll be right there," she told Dylan. "I want to check the computer log first. Make sure we haven't received any threatening messages."

Dylan nodded at her and gestured to Campbell. He stepped through the door right behind him.

Natasha glanced at the error log. No new messages. No changed files. No alerts. She set the alert at maximum volume, then joined the others.

"—this whole area," Mintz was saying as she entered and sat next to Dylan.

Mintz was holding a laser pointer and pointing to areas on a blueprint he'd tacked up onto the wall. A black marker border had been roughly drawn around the dining room, kitchen, play area and the section of wall that bordered the family quarters.

"We didn't see any damage in the west hallway," she commented.

"That's because the steel reinforcement did its job. I'm guessing the inside south walls may be cracked or even crumbling, but they held up, just like they were supposed to."

"How long will we be in lockdown, Alfred?" Dylan asked.

"I'm hoping a couple of days at the most. We have our landline and we're hardwired into the Internet. We can stay in communication with the FBI, my guards and local law enforcement. By the way—" he turned to Dylan "—I've sent the guards and the rest of the staff home. They're to check in every six hours with me."

"How do you reverse the lockdown?" Campbell asked in a shaky voice.

Natasha looked up. She wanted to know the answer to that question, too. Her pulse sped up.

Mintz sent Campbell a hard look. "Only four people can engage or disengage lockdown. That includes Dylan, Agent Rudolph, myself and Robby."

Campbell took a shaky breath. "So Robby can unlock the lab from above?"

Mintz shook his head. "Nope. This box is the only place the lockdown can be disengaged."

"What if—what if something happens down here. What if you three are hurt, or—" He swallowed and licked his lips. "I'll be trapped!" He stood, sending his chair rolling toward the wall.

"Calm down. Nobody's going to be hurt. The basement is fortified against attack."

Campbell wiped his face. "I've got to get out of here. I'm going to get that water."

As soon as he left, Mintz raised his brows at Dylan.

"He seems to be claustrophobic." He glanced at Natasha. "And paranoid." He sent a thoughtful glance toward the door. "Has he got reason? Is Campbell Tom's inside source?"

Chapter Eleven

Dylan blew his breath out in a harsh sigh. "I don't know if Campbell is the inside source or not. I'm getting mixed signals from him."

"Mixed how?" Mintz asked.

"I know what he means, sir," Natasha put in. "He's genuinely terrified, but is it claustrophobia, or something else? We have to consider that the next attack will be on the lab. And if Campbell is the hacker's accomplice, there's a chance he's set a trap, and he's panicking because he's afraid he won't be able to get out of here before the trap is sprung."

"We'll have to keep an eye on him," Mintz said.

"Alfred, are we okay on provisions?"

"We can support four people for twenty-eight days."

Natasha's stomach lurched. Her hands were clammy. She knew the fragile control she clung to was keeping her from acting just like Campbell. The ceiling felt as if it was straining with the weight of the dirt and metal above it. The rooms even seemed smaller.

Dylan stood. "I should keep practicing with the virtual surgery program. Let me know if anything happens. *Anything*."

Mintz nodded.

A beeping sound reached Natasha's ears.

Mintz and Dylan straightened, looking at each other.

"It's the alert—on my computer." She stood and headed for the door. "It's the hacker."

Mintz and Dylan followed her into her cubicle. She went straight to the computer and sat, studying the screen.

"He's sent an e-mail to you, Dylan," she said, as she quickly accessed the program that supported e-mail and instant messages for the household. The code scrolled slowly across the screen. She studied it, dreading what she would find.

There. She hit Scroll Lock on the keyboard. She was looking at the code Tom had sent. It was a real e-mail, but it had a hidden attachment.

She muttered a delicate curse under her breath. "He's sent a hidden attachment. If you'd opened the message, the attachment would have self-activated."

"What is it?" Dylan asked.

She looked up at him. "A worm.

"Can you read the e-mail?"

"I may be able to import it into the diagnostic program and decode it without touching the worm. I'll do it on the shell, just in case."

Dylan watched Natasha's slender fingers flying across the keyboard. On the monitor screen, all he saw were rows and rows of gibberish—letters and numbers and mathematical symbols. Nothing he recognized. No real words.

Campbell came in with a bottle of water. "I heard a beeping noise. What's going on now?" He walked up behind Natasha and leaned down to see the screen. "What are you doing? Did somebody try to access the system?" His voice sounded strained—or excited.

Dylan frowned. Campbell had been with him over a year and not once had Dylan suspected he was anything but a very talented programmer and loyal employee.

Natasha glanced at Dylan, drawing his gaze. He saw in her eyes that she was going to lie to Campbell. He inclined his head slightly in agreement.

"The beeping was an alert. I'm sweeping the system to be sure nothing happened." She swept them all with her gaze. "I'd really like to do this alone. The fewer distractions the better."

Dylan took the hint. "Jerry, I want to practice with the virtual surgery module. I'd like for you to run a few tests on the program, just to be sure there are no hidden bugs."

Campbell straightened. "Sure. It'll take my mind off the fact that I'm trapped down here."

"I'll check the provisions and verify that the lockdown's working like it's supposed to," Mintz said. He left the room and headed down the hall.

Dylan watched Natasha's face. She'd found something. "Go on," he said to Campbell. "I'll be right there."

Campbell eyed him and Natasha narrowly, but nodded. "Sure."

He exited Natasha's office and stepped across the hall to the virtual surgery lab. He could still see them if he looked their way, but he sat at his computer and began typing.

Dylan turned a side chair around and sat next to her, so he could see the screen. "Any luck?" he asked.

She glanced up and across the hall at Campbell, then shook her head. "Yep. Here's the text of Tom's e-mail."

Dylan scanned the words she pulled up on the screen.

DS—R U msng Ur boy? We cd arng a trade Ur kid for interface U got 1 hr N—watch out. I'm in.

"What does that mean? *Watch out. I'm in.*"

"That's to me. He's talking about the worm. But I've quarantined it."

"Quarantined it? Why not just delete it?"

Her slender shoulders shrugged. "I'd like to study it, see what he did. So far the things he's done are typical of any hacker worth his salt. He's planning something. If I can review the program he wrote, I can tell how much better he's gotten since I knew him. Maybe I can turn the tables on him, and get evidence to prosecute him."

But Dylan didn't care about Tom. He was willing to do anything, even give up the neural interface, to have Ben back in his arms, safe and sound.

"Send him an e-mail."

"What?" Natasha looked at him, wide-eyed. "You're not thinking of—"

"Send it. Tell him I'll give him the program if he'll let Ben go."

She turned toward him. He straightened and took his hand off the back of her chair.

"He won't let Ben go. It would be too dangerous for him. He's obviously insinuated himself into a domestic terrorist group—maybe even become their ersatz leader. He's very charismatic, very persuasive."

"Is that why you went to work for him?" He hadn't meant to say that, but her description of

Tom had ignited a spark inside him, a spark of jealousy. It shocked him that right now, in the midst of his worry for Ben's safety, that he could feel anything.

She frowned. "No. Even back then, naive as I was, I had better sense than to get involved with him. But I was just out of high school and broke. I'd gotten away from Children's Services on the day I turned eighteen."

Children's Services. A pang of pity dug into his heart.

She must have seen it in his eyes, because she lifted her chin and her green eyes sparkled defiantly. "Don't feel sorry for me. I did just fine."

But he knew that wasn't true. He knew she lay awake at night, frightened, because of how her parents had died. He knew that when she thought no one was looking, a haunted fear darkened her eyes.

A muscle worked under the pale, delicate skin of her jaw. She sent him a sidelong glance before looking back at the screen. Her hands were poised over the keyboard, and Dylan saw them trembling.

Heartsick for what she'd gone through, Dylan reached out and took her hand. She stiffened, but he held on, intertwining his fingers with hers and rubbing his thumb across the back of her hand.

She looked at their hands then at him. "I asked you not to feel sorry for me."

He gave her a little smile. "I don't. I'm thinking about that little girl and looking at the woman she's become."

Her cheeks turned pink. She slid her hand away from his. "I'd better get to work."

"Wait. You didn't tell me how you got tangled up with Tom."

Her attitude changed immediately. Her back straightened. "No, I didn't," she said coldly. "But in the interests of full disclosure—" she took a deep breath. "I was on the streets. Tom was recruiting. That means he was wandering through the areas where homeless people hung out and asking if anybody knew how to operate a computer. I said I did. He took me back to his apartment and gave me an assignment, to change the balance on his bank account. It took me about twenty minutes. He was impressed."

"So you are a hacker."

"Not now. Now I catch them."

"Then why haven't you caught Tom?" He heard the faint note of suspicion in his voice. But his son's life was depending on her. He had to know everything he could find out about her.

She pinned him with her sharp gaze. "He

knows I'm in the FBI. He's obviously avoided me. Plus, as I told you—he's very good."

"Better than you?"

"I hope not."

"So how did you go from homeless to the FBI?"

She didn't answer. She was studying the computer screen. "Damn it!" she said. She started typing, her fingers flying over the keyboard.

"What is it?" He saw code scrolling rapidly down the screen and a small pop-up window in the corner of the screen.

She shook her head. "His worm self-extracted."

"I thought you quarantined it."

"I did," she snapped. She hit the enter key twice, cursed under her breath and hit it one more time. She grimaced and started typing again.

"It's gaining speed."

"Can't we turn the damn thing off? Stop him that way?"

"Call Mintz."

Dylan unhooked the mobile radio from his waistband and pressed Alfred's shortcut key. "Alfred, get in here. Tasha's workstation."

"If we turn the system off, the UPS will kick in." She glanced up. "Uninterruptible power source. It will probably take twenty minutes or so for it to shut down."

Alfred came running up the hall, carrying the specially built box that held the completed interface implant. Dylan opened the door for him.

"Good. You brought it."

Alfred nodded. "You sounded serious. I figure it's better to keep it with us. What's up?"

Campbell appeared from the lab. "What's going on?" he said. He was decidedly pale.

"The hacker sent a self-extracting worm."

"Oh, crap," Campbell muttered, fiddling with his ponytail.

Alfred looked at Natasha. "Agent Rudolph? What do you recommend?"

She met his gaze. "How long do the servers take to completely shut down?"

Alfred's dark eyes narrowed. "Twenty-three minutes."

"And self-destruct?"

"Eight minutes. But that destroys everything."

Dylan looked from one to the other. "You can't do that."

"If we don't, Tom and his terrorists will have the interface."

Dylan considered his choices. They could start the system shutdown and take the chance that Tom's worm would take longer than twenty-three minutes to infiltrate the secure area of the server.

Or they could destroy everything he owned, everything he'd worked for, in eight minutes.

He looked at the box that contained the tiny prototype interface implant and two disks containing programming instructions and requirements, and mapping information.

He'd be leaving behind all his research, notes and the preliminary research on an even smaller implant using nanotechnology and state-of-the-art magnifying technology. Years of work.

"What's that window in the corner of your screen?" he asked her.

She looked. "It's a message from Tom. '*U got 5 min.*'"

Regret sat on his chest like a weight. There was only one decision. They had to destroy the house and the lab. He turned to Alfred. "Do it."

Alfred nodded and handed Dylan the box.

"Do what?" Campbell's horrified gaze took in the three of them.

"You three," Alfred said, "get into the tunnel with the interface. I'll set the timer."

Natasha was still at the computer.

"How does it look?" Dylan asked.

"Not good. I've slowed it down a little by setting barriers, but it's speeding up and I can't stay ahead of it much longer."

"You can't destroy the house. We'll be stuck

down here." Campbell grabbed Alfred's arm. "Call him. Give him everything! It's not worth our lives!"

"Calm down, Campbell. You don't have a choice. You're with us."

"I can't! I can't do it!" Campbell shoved Alfred and turned on Dylan. "You've got to let me out of here!"

Dylan grabbed him and slammed him up against the wall. "We don't have time for this," he said through clenched teeth. "Alfred, there are some plastic lock-ties in the drawer under the pad and stylus in there." He indicated the virtual surgery lab. "Grab the longest ones."

"What the hell are you going to do?" Campbell squeaked.

"I'm going to cuff you if you don't calm down."

"You wouldn't."

Dylan pressed his forearm against Campbell's throat. "Try me."

Campbell stared, wide-eyed, at Dylan. He felt Campbell's throat move as he swallowed. After a few seconds, the bioengineer quit fighting. He relaxed and held up his hands in a gesture of surrender. His face poured sweat and his whole body trembled. "I'll be okay," he croaked.

Alfred came back into Natasha's office, carrying the plastic ties.

"Hold on to those in case we need them," Dylan said.

"You got it. Now, get out of here," Alfred said. "Let me set the destruct."

"Is the house empty?"

"I took a look at the security cameras a few minutes ago, and called Robby on the landline. He says everybody's gone. They plan to be back tomorrow to assess the damage and go through the debris."

"Good." Dylan met Alfred's gaze and held it. "Take Campbell and go on ahead. Get out as fast as you can and call the FBI to pick us up. You go with them, Tasha. I'll set the self-destruct and be right behind you."

Alfred opened his mouth, but Dylan held up a hand and let his gaze flicker toward Campbell. "I need you to do this, Alfred." *Don't let Campbell get away.*

His old friend frowned, then nodded. "Okay."

Dylan blew out a breath in relief. Alfred had gotten the message.

"Tasha?"

She shook her head. "I need to keep throwing up barriers as long as possible. Every one of them buys us a few seconds. I'll go when you go."

He started to argue, but this time it was Alfred

sending him a silent message. With a sigh, he acquiesced. She and Alfred were right. They could use every second they could buy.

Alfred took Campbell by the arm. "Let's you and me get out of here."

Campbell went reluctantly. "How long is the tunnel?"

Alfred was answering him as they headed into the access room.

"Do you think Campbell is the accomplice?" Natasha asked, without looking up from the screen.

"Do you?"

She shook her head. "I don't think he has the— you know." She sent him a fleeting smile.

Dylan couldn't help but laugh a little. "Right. I agree. But I don't think we can take a chance. Alfred's treating him like a suspect until we can prove otherwise." He gestured toward the door. "I'm going across the hall to set the self-destruct. We'll have thirty seconds before the explosions start. Be ready in fifteen seconds."

She nodded, still typing so fast the clicks blended into one sound.

In the briefing room he opened the box and pulled the red lever labeled Self-Destruct Do Not Touch. Then he hurried back into Natasha's office and grabbed the box that held the interface.

"Let's go."

She typed a few more lines, then stood and kicked her chair backward, still typing.

He grabbed her arm. "Now!"

She straightened, but didn't take her eyes off the computer screen. "It's still gaining strength. I should have been able to stop it."

"Ten seconds, Tasha."

Together they stepped into the anteroom. Dylan scanned his print and entered the pass code. He took her hand.

"Ready?"

Her throat moved as she swallowed. Her face was set. Her wide eyes met his gaze.

God, he wished he could do something to alleviate her fear. He'd told Campbell the truth about the tranquilizers. He did have some, but they were back in the lab.

"Come on," he said. "We'll be through the tunnel and out in no time."

She nodded, but doubt and worry were still etched on her face.

He squeezed her fingers and pulled her through the door.

Natasha swallowed the scream that was pushing up from her chest. Panic reverberated in her head and her throat constricted.

She felt the tons of dirt over her head. She

smelled soot and smoke and dust and felt her lungs straining for air.

She knew her memory was playing tricks on her senses, sending her back to the worst moments of her life. But knowing didn't take away the panic.

As the heavy metal door swung shut behind them, Natasha gasped and closed her eyes to keep from looking back at it.

"Hey." Dylan's fingers squeezed hers reassuringly. "Calm down. You're cutting off the circulation in my fingers."

"Sorry," she said, loosening her grip. She was embarrassed at how small and quivery her voice sounded, how shaky her limbs were.

A deep rumble echoed in her ears, at first almost too quiet to notice, but gaining in strength and noise. To her left, she heard something creak. The lights in front of her flickered and dust fell from the ceiling.

"The explosions," she squeaked. "They're going to collapse the tunnel."

Chapter Twelve

Natasha covered her mouth to stop the scream that was clawing its way up her throat. Her scalp burned. Her hands quivered. If she didn't get hold of herself within a few seconds she'd collapse, paralyzed with terror.

Quiet and safe. Plenty of fresh air. Breathe. Breathe. Breathe. The mantra's words did their job. They evoked a sliver of assurance.

"The tunnel won't collapse. Alfred is an explosives expert. It's what he did in the military. He's built this place to practically withstand a nuclear attack. I can assure you that he's built protection into the tunnel. I trust Alfred with my life."

She nodded. "Then—then I do, too."

As they continued down the corridor, her eyes hungrily sought each dim circle of light. They helped, but she was ready to be at the other end of the dark passage. And the fact that the muffled rumbling continued didn't help.

"Dylan, I'm sorry. I'd give anything not to be like this."

"There's nothing to apologize for. I admire you."

She glanced at his face, which was planed in shadow. "Admire?" She laughed bitterly. "After what I did to you?"

He stopped her with a touch on her upper arm. "Listen to me, Tasha. You are one of the bravest people I've ever known."

"Brave? Look at me. I'm a mess."

His face, harshly beautiful in the dim light and shadows and his intense blue eyes made him look like a dark angel.

"And yet you're here."

"I wouldn't be without you."

His face changed, softened, and she saw a look in his eyes that she'd seen a time or two before. But she couldn't quite interpret it.

It was almost tender, almost loving. Or was it just pity? A surge of emotion flooded her—gratitude, relief, mixed with a peculiar longing she hardly recognized. For an instant they overpowered her barely contained panic.

She recalled her first impression of Dylan. Intense, exuding masculinity. Her heart flipped in her chest as a different kind of panic overtook her.

She was falling in love with him.

Her breath caught in her throat. *No.* She refused to let that happen. He was obsessed with his child. He had no love left over for her.

Besides, that was one of the first things Decker had taught her. Falling for a victim was unacceptable—frowned on by the FBI. It was also against her own principles.

As soon as they found Ben, Dylan and he would be whisked off to one of NSA's untraceable secure facilities, and she'd go back to her sunny apartment and the job that had once meant everything to her.

"Tell me what you're thinking," Dylan said.

She shook her head. "Nothing. How far is it to the shack?"

His mouth quirked up. "We're about halfway. We need to hurry." He let go of her arms and started walking. Despite her long legs, she had trouble keeping up with him.

"Are Mintz and Campbell waiting for us?"

"I hope not. Alfred should have taken the car and driven into town, so Detective Buckram can put Campbell in custody until we get Ben back."

"Can Mintz handle him?"

"Oh, yeah," he said firmly. "Remember when you said Campbell wasn't in very good shape? Well, Alfred works out in the exercise room and runs every day. He could probably beat up any of his men."

"That's good." She caught herself counting the lights. "Dylan, when we get out, we need to contact Storm. Find out the latest on Ben, and get you and the interface to a safe house."

"We'll definitely get the latest on Ben, but I won't be going to a safe house."

"You have to. Your safety and the safety of your interface are too important."

He stopped and turned. "What I have to do is find Ben."

"We will. I promise you. We will."

He started walking again. Natasha skipped and lengthened her stride to keep up.

Then as they rounded a gentle curve, she saw the tiny red circle of light in the midst of the white ones. "There's the exit." A sigh of relief escaped her lips.

"You made it," Dylan said, glancing back at her and nodding his head.

"Yeah." She smiled at him. "Thanks to you."

"Well, isn't that sweet."

Natasha froze. Just ahead of her, Dylan stopped in his tracks.

Fear washed over her like scalding water. *Tom.* She'd never forget that sarcastic voice. Her gaze swept the thirty or so feet between her and the door.

Tom stood in the corner opposite the door, dressed in black. If he hadn't moved or spoken, they wouldn't have seen him until they were almost to the door.

Dylan put out a hand to shield her. She measured the distance from where she stood to Tom. Too far to lunge.

She stood about two feet behind Dylan. She felt the weight of her Glock in her fanny pack. If she stayed back, she might be able to get her pack unzipped and retrieve her weapon.

"Hello, Natasha," Tom said. "Long time, eh? Dr. Stryker, it's a pleasure to meet you at last."

Dylan didn't speak.

"Did Natasha tell you that she and I are colleagues?"

Natasha felt Dylan stiffen beside her, but he kept quiet. Her pulse hammered in her throat and ears. Did Dylan still doubt her?

"That's right. We've worked together before. Haven't we Natasha? Those were good times, weren't they?"

"How did you get in here?" she snapped.

Tom laughed. "Are you kidding me? I practically walked right in. Not that this isn't a nice little secret exit. Unfortunately—" he grinned "—your abandoned road and the empty house are visible on aerial photos of the area. Especially photos from ten years ago, when it wasn't so overgrown."

"I don't know what you think you're going to accomplish—"

"Oh, honey." Tom gestured and Natasha saw his gun. She was surprised. He'd never carried a gun before—at least not that she knew about. Of course what she didn't know about Tom would fill a very big book. She'd never even known where he lived.

"I'm taking the interface. It will bring millions—possibly even billions—on the foreign market. I've already got several government leaders interested."

Dylan spoke. "I don't have it. It's back there. I destroyed it with the house."

"Right. And what's that in your hand? Your lunch?" Tom laughed out loud, then waved his gun at Dylan. "Set it on the floor and slide it over here with your foot."

Natasha felt a change in Dylan's stance. Fear arrowed through her. He was going to try to rush Tom.

He'd be killed.

"Dylan," she muttered.

"Well, well, listen to you." Tom didn't take his eyes off Dylan as he spoke to her. "You got a little crush on your doctor? It sounds like it to me. Why don't you use your persuasive powers to convince him that it's in his best interest to hand over the box."

"I wouldn't dream of telling Dr. Stryker what to do."

"Let's go, Stryker. You're wasting precious time. Time your child doesn't have."

Dylan held the metal box in one hand as he bent his knees. Then suddenly he hurled the box, underhanded, at Tom.

Tom jerked to one side and the box crashed against the stone walls. His face distorted in anger. He clutched his gun in both hands and walked a few steps closer to them.

"That was an incredibly stupid move!" he shouted. "What the hell's the matter with you? That machine better be packed well."

Dylan shrugged and held out his hands in a submissive gesture. "I told you, it's not the interface."

"And I told you I don't believe you." Tom dug into his pants pocket and pulled out a cell phone. "See this, Doc? This is my direct line to the person who's holding Ben. If I don't call within one hour to stop them, they have instructions to kill him."

Dylan stared at the man who held his son's life in his hands. He wanted to rush him and beat him within an inch of his life, gun be damned. If he could overpower him, he could get the cell phone and the FBI could trace the calls.

"I don't believe *you*," he said. "You have your

supposed interface. What are you going to do with us?"

"Why, I'm going to kill you. What else?" Tom looked genuinely surprised that he hadn't figured that out.

"Why don't you just lock us in here and get away with your precious box? And let my son go."

Tom eyed him narrowly, then nudged the box with his foot.

"Why don't you open the box for me?" His gaze snapped to Natasha. "But first. Natasha, my dear, please unhook your fanny pack—with your left hand. I want to see your right hand in the air."

Natasha glanced at Dylan then complied. She had a little trouble manipulating the catch, but finally popped it. She tried to catch the pack, but couldn't with one hand. It thudded to the floor.

Tom grinned, his eyes darting from her to Dylan then back. "So, you *were* armed. Put both hands up. Now kick the pack over here."

She did what he asked. Dylan could tell by her face that she was racking her brain to think of a way to overpower Tom.

Tom reached out with one foot and dragged the fanny pack closer. "Now, Doc. How 'bout we open the box?"

He kicked the metal box carefully so that it slid

to a stop a foot from Dylan's shoe. "And don't try anything else or I'll be forced to put a hole in sweet Natasha's forehead. And it would be such a shame to mar that lovely face."

Dylan's jaw ached with tension and anger. He had to figure out how to stop Tom. He and Natasha should be able to overpower the skinny, puffy-faced little man. But Tom seemed awfully comfortable with the big semiautomatic he wielded. And it was a very good, very accurate gun. A Desert Eagle. It underscored the theory that Tom was fraternizing with a terrorist group.

With that firepower in his hand, there was no way he or Natasha would survive a point-blank shot.

He began to crouch down to reach the box.

"Hold it. Put your right hand in your pocket, and bend at the waist. Open the box with one hand. Natasha, back away. Two steps."

"The latch makes it impossible to open one-handed."

"Give it up, Doc. I'm not buying any of your flimsy efforts to slow me down. And by the way, time's a-wastin' for your kid."

Ben. He did what Tom said. He'd told him the truth about the box's latch, but by holding the box steady with his foot, he managed to get it open.

"Straighten up and kick it back to me. And if

you try anything this time, I *will* shoot her. I don't need her anymore and I'm not very fond of her these days."

Tom glanced down at the open box, then grinned at him. "What do you know. It *is* the implant, isn't it? And DVDs. Instructions for programming I hope."

"Now you've got what you wanted. Take it and tell me where my son is."

Natasha moved back to his side. "Come on, Tom. You're home free. You disappeared before. You can do it again."

"Natasha," Dylan said. "Do something for me. Tell him you won't ID him. I just want to get my son back." He glared at Tom. "I don't give a damn what happens to you, but I'm willing to keep quiet if you'll just give me my son unharmed. He means more to me than any technology."

"I do," Natasha said to Tom. "I do promise. I swear. Please let Ben go."

Tom smirked. "You don't get it do you? I'm not through with you. You defied me. So high and mighty, not wanting to hack into the government's files. Are you still as idealistic and naive as you were? Come on. The government is corrupt. Why not steal their secrets. You even skated on the prison time. I can't believe you got a job with the

FBI for *hacking* them!" He shook his head. "Inside the FBI. We could have been rich."

Dylan listened in fascination. He finally understood exactly what had happened to Natasha eight years ago. She'd tried to tell him, but he'd been so angry, so worried about Ben that he hadn't paid attention to her.

She'd been framed by Tom, betrayed by him.

"Tom, please. Whatever you're going to do—do it. Take me with you. If you'll let Ben go, I'll go with you. I'll work for you."

"No!" *Crap.* He hadn't meant to blurt that out. He clamped his mouth shut.

Tom's dark eyes sparkled. "You'll work for me? You're falling on your sword for his kid? And, you…" He turned to Dylan. "I guess you can't stand to think of her working for me, can you?"

He laughed loud and long. "I see what's going on now. You two are in love, aren't you?" He shook his head. "Sorry, Natasha. I appreciate the offer, but you'll understand why I can't bring myself to trust you."

Dylan studied him, waiting for an opportunity to jump him. He wasn't concerned about himself, although he'd rather not die here. His main concern was Natasha. He knew that even if Tom killed him, she'd do everything humanly possible to save Ben.

"But before I do anything—permanent—one of you open this door for me. I haven't touched it, figuring you probably have some kind of lockout on it." Tom looked at Natasha. "Come open the door."

"She doesn't have access," Dylan snapped, hoping to hell that Natasha would keep quiet.

"Doc, would you give me a break? You're becoming so freaking annoying that I feel like shooting you just to shut you up."

Dylan shrugged. "Let her try then. As you said, there's a lockout for incorrect entries."

"Then you get over here. Natasha, turn your face to the wall and put your hands up. High up, palms against the wall."

Dylan saw Natasha comply. The awkward pose raised her top to her midriff, exposing a lot of skin between her ribs and her hips in the low-rise jeans she wore.

He moved slowly toward Tom, his hands spread. As he approached, Tom kept the gun aimed at his head. He didn't have any idea if his impromptu plan was smart or stupid, but it was all he could come up with.

"Go ahead. Enter your code."

"I have to get my pass code generator out of my pocket. It's on that chain that's attached to my belt."

Tom pressed the barrel of the gun into the nape

of his neck. "Go ahead. If it's not your pass code device, then it's bye-bye, Doc."

He slipped the pass code generator out of his pocket and held it so Tom could see it. The pressure of the gun barrel against his skin relaxed a little.

"Okay, Doc. Your kid's waiting. Let's go."

For an instant, Dylan's anguished heart wanted to believe Tom. That all he was going to do was take the interface. That as soon as he was safely away from the shack, he'd call and tell his accomplice to let Ben go.

But looking into his eyes, Dylan knew with a sick dread that Tom wasn't like that. He was the type who didn't want a mess. Natasha, Ben and he were a mess that Tom would want to clean up.

So he used his middle finger instead of his thumb in the fingerprint reader, then entered the numbers that appeared on the tiny screen of the pass code generator.

The lock flashed red and beeped.

"I thought you didn't touch the lock," Dylan burst out before Tom had a chance to react. "Damn, what did you do?"

"What the hell?" Tom buried a centimeter of the gun barrel into Dylan's neck. A shooting pain streaked up his skull. "I didn't do anything. I swear, Doc. If you don't get that door open, I'll shoot you both right now."

Dylan nodded and met Tom's gaze. "You *have* to tell me if you did anything to the lock." He knew he looked scared to death. He just hoped Tom would think it was because of the lock rather than fear that Tom would shoot them if the door didn't open.

Tom blinked and scowled. "I didn't do anything."

"You didn't press any of the buttons? You didn't try your fingerprint?"

"I might have accidentally touched the keypad. What the hell are you saying?"

"Quiet!" Dylan said. "If I don't enter the correct code within twenty seconds—" He tried it again, still using the wrong finger on the print reader.

The lights flashed red and the beeping started again.

"Ah, hell." He allowed the panic that swirled inside him to seep into his voice. "I only have one more chance," he lied.

Tom pushed him against the wall and put the gun barrel under his chin. "Get the damn door open or you're both dead."

Dylan lifted his chin. "If you kill us you'll never get out."

"I swear I'll kill you." He cocked the gun.

At the same time the snick of metal against metal echoed around the tunnel. A solid whine began and immediately rose in pitch and blared.

Dylan took a deep breath, prepared to grab Tom's gun.

Behind him, Natasha screamed.

Tom froze, his finger on the trigger.

"No! Dylan!" she cried, reaching out, touching the concrete walls. "I can't stand it. Get me out of here." She beat her fists against the walls. "Get me out! Get me out! Oh, God! I can't breathe!" She collapsed to the ground.

Taking advantage of the distraction, Dylan shoved Tom with all his might.

A gunshot rang out.

NATASHA JUMPED UP and dived toward the two men who were in a deadlock against the wall. Her ears rang with the sound of the gunshot. Her heart pounded in terror. Was Dylan shot?

As she reached them, Tom shoved Dylan away. Blood smeared them both, but the dark red stuff bloomed and spread on Dylan's shirt.

Oh no! Dylan looked stunned.

She wanted to go to him, check him, stop the bleeding. But her training had taught her to neutralize the threat first.

She lowered her head and rammed Tom in the belly, then flung her arms upward, hoping to disarm him. But his skinny pallid appearance hid a wiry strength. She knocked the breath out of him with her head-butt, but he didn't fall. He kicked her, bruising her shin.

Then pain exploded in her head.

She blinked and suddenly found herself flat on the floor.

"Tasha!"

Dylan's voice echoed in her head. He sounded as if he was in a tunnel. She squeezed her eyes shut and quelled the urge to laugh. He *was* in a tunnel.

Damn it. She shook her head. She was dazed from Tom's blow. She got her arms and legs under her and tried to push herself up.

"Look at me, Natasha," Tom said.

She looked at his shoes. He was standing right in front of her and she knew he was pointing his gun at her head.

He nudged her with his foot. "Look at me! I want to see your face when you die."

She rose to her hands and knees and took a deep breath, preparing to slam into his knees. She wanted to check on Dylan, but she didn't dare take the time. She needed all her concentration, all her strength, to try to save her life and his.

She raised her head slowly and tensed, preparing to ram her shoulder into his knees. Her heart hammered in her chest.

But a shadow loomed over her and Tom went down.

Dylan. He'd slammed Tom against the wall and was pummeling him with his fist.

Tom was doing his best to keep the gun out of Dylan's reach. He waved his gun arm high in the air. Dylan was right on top of him so he couldn't get the gun in between them. A shot rang out but it went wild.

Wincing at the deafening report, Natasha grabbed Tom's wrist in both hands, but both men fell toward her, and she lost her grip.

As she scrambled out of the way to try again to disarm him, she realized his arms were no longer flailing. He'd gotten them between him and Dylan. They were struggling for control of the gun.

She watched in horror, not breathing. *Please. Get the gun,* she screamed silently at Dylan.

Dylan's face was pale and covered in sweat. He was losing strength fast.

She cast about, looking for something to use as a weapon. Something to help Dylan. Her eyes lit on the metal box. She picked it up and rushed the two men, aiming to hit Tom on the head.

The gun went off.

All three of them froze. Dylan and Tom's faces reflected surprise and fear.

Natasha's heart thudded once against her chest then seemed to stop.

"Dylan," she sobbed, reaching for him.

He turned his eyes toward her, then closed them.

"No, no, no," she whispered. "Don't die. Oh God, please. Don't let him die."

He took a step backward and she saw the gun in his hands.

Tom looked at her, his eyes barely focused. "Natasha," he muttered. "We could have ruled the world." Blood was turning his black shirt darker, wetter.

He looked down and touched the wet material then looked at his blood-smeared hand.

"Still the best," he whispered, then crumpled where he stood. His head thudded loudly against the concrete floor.

Dylan dropped the gun. He looked stunned.

"Your shoulder," Natasha said, rushing to his side.

"Yeah, I'm kind of shot."

"Kind of?" She hiccoughed a little laugh.

He lifted his good hand and swiped his thumb across her cheeks. "Don't cry, Tasha."

"I'm not crying." She shook her head. "FBI agents don't cry."

"Yeah right." He stepped away from her, toward Tom. He leaned down and briefly laid his fingers against Tom's throat. "He's dead." He looked up at her. "I killed him."

"Self-defense."

He blinked and his blue eyes sharpened to

electric blue. He turned over Tom's body and fel in his pockets. "His cell phone." He stood swaying a bit.

Natasha looked at the screen as he thumbe through the recent numbers. Most calls were t one number. So he pressed the call button. But th screen brought up a No Service message.

"Damn it!" He stepped over closer to the doo and tried again. "No service in here."

He looked down the tunnel back toward th lab. "We've got to get out of here. Ben's runnin; out of time."

"There should be an escape route."

Dylan looked stricken. "This *is* the escap route." He rubbed his hand down his face.

"What about an override for the doors?"

"Sure. In an hour, but by then whoever has Be will have—" His voice shook.

"You're telling me Mintz didn't build an escap hatch on this tunnel?"

Dylan nodded. He wiped his eyes.

"That's not possible. Mintz wouldn't take th chance of getting locked in here." It didn't mak sense, given Mintz's insistence on triple redun dancy. "Come on, let's find it."

"Might as well," he said. "I don't have a bette idea." He looked around, then rubbed his temple

'Where's the box?" His voice was strained and his face was pale.

"Over here." She picked it up. "I need to wrap your shoulder. You're losing a lot of blood."

He looked down at the bloody T-shirt. "No time. Let's go. I don't think we have but about thirty minutes."

She nodded. Ben's life was at stake.

They walked back up the tunnel, examining every inch of wall. "This is taking too long," she said. "If I were Alfred, where would I put an escape?"

"In the middle?"

"That's what I was thinking. Now, where's the middle?"

"Right before the first curve. We're pretty close." Dylan was sounding more and more strained and his voice was getting weaker. He took out the cell phone and tried it again. "Still no signal," he mumbled.

Natasha slipped under his good shoulder and wrapped an arm around his waist. "Lean on me," she said.

He tried not to but soon he was allowing her to help him walk. "Here's the curve. The midpoint of the tunnel is about fifty feet from here. God, I hope we're right."

As they walked around the curve, Natasha counted her steps.

Just then, she heard a faint noise.

"Did you hear that?" she asked. "Wait!" Sh
stopped. Did she feel air? Fresh air? "I think
feel a breeze."

Just then dirt and sand sifted onto the floor.

"Dylan!" A gruff, unmistakable voice echoe
in the tunnel.

Dylan looked around, hope striking a spark i
his eyes. "Alfred?"

"Dylan! Natasha! Answer me!"

The words echoed all around them.

"Alfred!" Dylan's voice broke. "Thank God."

Natasha studied the wall on the north side of th
corridor. There, about four feet from the floo
was a section of concrete that didn't look like th
rest, on close examination. She tapped on it. I
sounded hollow.

"Dylan!"

It *was* Mintz. "Stand back," he shouted.

A noise like a fist hitting a wall reverberate
through the tunnel. Then a second blow followe
the first, and Mintz's fist slammed throug
drywall that had been painted to look lik
concrete. Light and air gushed in through the hol
blowing drywall dust into their faces.

A shadow blocked the light as Mintz poked hi
head in through the hole.

"Dylan's injured." Natasha took the metal bo
from Dylan's hand and handed it to Mintz.

"Gambrini's right behind me."

"Dylan—" she squeezed his waist "—give me Tom's cell phone."

He leaned against the wall and fished it from his pocket. "Find Ben," he muttered.

"We will. Here." She handed the phone to Mintz and called out to Gambrini.

"The last called number is to whoever's holding Ben. They have instructions to kill Ben in probably fifteen or twenty minutes if Tom doesn't call them."

Mintz handed the phone behind him. "Where is Tom?"

"He won't be calling anybody." Dylan's words were slurred. "Find him, Alfred. Find Ben."

"I'll take care of it, sir," Gambrini said.

Natasha heard him scrambling backward, out of the tunnel.

Dylan slumped. "Alfred, Dylan's passing out. He's lost too much blood."

"Gambrini," Mintz called over his shoulder. "Send Robby and Hector in here and phone an ambulance *now*. We've got to get Dylan out of there."

"No," Dylan mumbled as he slid down the wall. "No ambu…lance. Ben. Save…Ben."

Chapter Thirteen

Natasha rode in the ambulance with Dylan. She wanted to go with Mintz to join Storm and Gambrini in rescuing Ben, but Mintz had refused to let her.

"He'll need you when he wakes up," he'd told her.

"He'll need you more," she retorted. "He trusts you."

Mintz had met her gaze solemnly. "But he loves you."

Now she paced the short length of the emergency room cubicle with Mintz's words echoing in her ears as she waited for Dylan to wake up. Stopping at the head of the bed, she pushed a damp strand of hair off his forehead and picked up the cool, wet towel the nurse had given her. She patted his face.

He groaned, but didn't open his eyes.

She traced his honed jaw, his cheekbone, his brow. His pallor and weakness brought tears to her eyes. He was so determined, so focused. He was going to hate being injured.

She looked at the bandage covering his shoulder and part of his neck. An awful realization hit her.

Oh, dear God! His shoulder. He couldn't operate on Ben.

"No, please," she prayed. "Don't let Ben lose his chance to walk." What had the doctor told her? That they'd know within twelve hours if he'd have to have surgery to repair ligaments. Without surgery it would take him at least two weeks to be able to use his arm. With surgery it would be more like six weeks.

Ben didn't have six weeks. He didn't even have two.

Natasha compressed her lips, trying not to cry. What would Dylan do? He'd said Ben probably only had about another week before he lost too much viable muscle and nerve tissue.

She remembered him saying there were only two other surgeons in the world that could do the delicate procedure that would give Ben the ability to walk.

She took out her cell phone and called Mitch Decker.

"Mitch, it's Natasha."

"Hey. Storm told me what happened. Are you okay?"

"Sure, I'm fine. Dylan's in the hospital and Storm and Alfred and several agents are looking for Ben. Mitch, that's not why I called." She took a deep breath. "Do you have any idea who Mohan Patel is? He's at the University of Mumbai. Or Frederick Werner at Johns Hopkins?"

"No, why?"

"Dylan's been shot in the shoulder. He can't operate on his son. He told me those two were the only other surgeons in the world who could do this operation. I need to get in touch with one of them."

There was a pause on the other end of the line, then she heard paper rustling.

"I know the Chief of Medicine at Johns Hopkins. Let me give him a call."

"Really? You'd do that?"

"Tell me the name again."

"Frederick Werner. Neurosurgeon. Dylan studied under him."

"Give me a few minutes."

"Mitch—thanks."

She disconnected and stared at the cell phone display. No calls. Why hadn't Alfred called? She was so worried about Ben.

Dylan's thick black eyelashes fluttered and he groaned again. "Ben?" he said hoarsely.

She set her phone on the bedside table, pasted

on a smile and leaned over the side rail. "Hi, there," she said, caressing his hair, working to put a light tone in her voice.

He frowned drowsily at her. "What's going on?" He went to push himself up and discovered that his arm was immobilized. "What the hell?"

"Tom shot you, remember?"

He let his head fall back against the pillows. "Tom shot me. When—?" He broke off.

Natasha saw his eyes sharpen as adrenaline overcame the effects of the morphine they'd given him.

"Where's Ben?"

"Dylan—"

"Damn it, Tasha." He glared at her. "Where is he? Where's Alfred?"

She put a hand on his chest. "They're looking for him. We should hear something soon."

"What are you doing here? Why aren't you out there helping them? Ben's going to—he'll be scared."

"Alfred made me promise to stay here with you."

He frowned at her, obviously assessing whether to believe her. "Are you telling me the truth? Or are you here because—because Ben—"

"No! No, Dylan. They've traced Tom's last call. Alfred and Storm and several other agents are on their way to the location now."

He closed his eyes and wiped his face with his good hand. "Swear to me you're telling the truth." He turned his searing gaze on her.

"I swear. I wouldn't lie to you."

"*Again,* you mean."

She compressed her lips. "I'm so sorry I didn't tell you about Tom earlier. I know if I had, Ben might not have been abducted."

"You can't know that."

"I've been going over everything, trying to figure out what went wrong. How someone inside the house could know where Ben was being hidden—" She stopped and met Dylan's gaze.

His eyes widened.

"Charlene," they said in unison.

"Oh my gosh, of course. It makes perfect sense." She pressed the heel of her hand against her temple. "How did I miss that? It's so obvious. Tom suckered her in, used her. Just like he used everybody—the young insurgents who did his dirty work for him, the homeless kids who believed that he would take care of them. I'm sure she thought he loved her. I've seen him in action. He had an incredible charisma when he wanted to turn it on. It's like he hypnotized his followers."

"Charlene. She wouldn't kill Ben, would she? I believe she truly cares for him."

"I'm sure she wouldn't." She pulled out her cell phone. "I need to make sure Mintz knows."

Dylan sank back against the pillows, obviously weak. It hurt her to see him injured.

She dialed Mintz's cell phone and quickly told him their revelation.

Dylan lay back on the pillows and tried not to think about what would happen to Ben if Charlene had been brainwashed by Tom. He concentrated on Natasha's voice as she talked with Mintz.

As soon as she hung up, he tried to sit up. The pain in his shoulder warned him about moving it too much. "What did he say?"

"They're at the hotel, just about to make contact. He said he'd come to the same conclusion—that Charlene was in on it."

"Do you think he's all right?"

She laid her hand on his wrist, just below the tape that held the IV line in place. "Yes, I do."

Slowly, he shook his head. "What if they don't find him? I need to be there when Alfred finds him. He won't understand why I'm not there," he said brokenly. "I can't—I can't—" He put his good hand over his face.

She stood and pushed his hair back off his forehead, then kissed his brow. "I know," she whispered, pressing her cheek against his.

Dylan breathed in her soft familiar scent. It reminded him of Ben's fresh bubble bath smell and his chest tightened with an aching loss.

He nudged her out of his way and struggled to sit up. "I've got to get up."

"Dylan, where do you think you're going? You can't get up. You're on a morphine drip, which you can control by pushing that button to give yourself a higher dose if you want. You have to lie still for twelve hours and you have to use the morphine. If you can stay still, they're hoping they won't have to do surgery to repair the ligaments."

Dylan glared down at the bandage and the tape that bound his arm to his ribs. The shoulder ached with a dull, persistent pain that made him feel queasy. He swallowed and licked his dry lips.

Natasha held a cup of water for him. He reached for it with his right hand, but the bandages and the IV line restrained him.

A shadow flickered in her green eyes as she held the straw for him to drink.

He stared down at his bandaged shoulder. "I can't do this. I can't lie here for twelve hours. I have to be ready to operate on Ben. Where's the interface?"

"Campbell has it. He looked at it and said it's fine." She sent him a questioning look. "Why'd you throw it at Tom? You could have broken it."

He gave her a sad smile. "I didn't care. At that moment nothing was more important than finding Ben. I'd have given my own life if I could trust Tom to set Ben free." He took a deep breath and blew it out. "I can build another interface. Ben is my only son."

Natasha sat beside his bed, her fingers making little pleats in the edge of the sheet that covered him. She'd showered and changed into a surgical scrub shirt and pants. Her hair was damp and tied up into a ponytail.

His gaze ran down her cheek to her jaw and on over her long graceful neck. Her skin glowed and her slender body looked sexy in the scrubs.

A tear slid down her cheek. She cared about Ben, too. Was worried about him.

Something happened inside him—something sweet and painful, comforting and frightening. He realized that as much as he loved Ben, his heart obviously had the capacity to love Natasha, too. Because he couldn't imagine living his life without her. He wanted to reach out and stop the tear but he couldn't—not with his right arm.

"Tasha, what's wrong?"

She shook her head without looking up.

Dylan saw her bowed shoulders, her pale face, and everything she'd told him sank in.

He'd been shot in the shoulder. He might have to have surgery.

"I can't operate on Ben." He heard his voice break.

She looked up, her fingers still playing with the sheet. The look in her eyes told him what he didn't want to know.

"I'm so sorry," she said. "I tried—"

He leaned back and closed his eyes and covered them with his good arm.

Natasha's cell phone rang.

"Mitch?" Her voice sounded anxious.

Dylan lay there, half listening. Her boss was probably talking to her about her next assignment.

"Really?" she said, her voice rising. "When can he be here?"

Dylan lowered his arm and opened his eyes.

"Tomorrow? That's great. Oh, Mitch, I can't tell you—" She paused. "Right. Thank you, sir."

She closed her phone and smiled at him.

"What was that?"

Her eyes sparkled with tears as she put her hand over his. "My boss, Mitch Decker, just talked to the Chief of Medicine at Johns Hopkins, who assured him that Dr. Frederick Werner can be here tomorrow to make arrangements to operate on Ben." By the time she'd finished, tears were streaming down her cheeks.

Dylan stared at her. "How? Why?"

"You told me he was one of only two other men who could do the operation."

He nodded, but terror gnawed at his gut.

"He'll be here. He can do the operation. You can—consult, or whatever it is you'd do." Natasha frowned. "What's the matter?"

"You think you've fixed everything? You got some strings pulled and you think that's going to solve all the problems? Sure, Werner can do the operation. Everything's rosy now."

"What's wrong with you? I thought you'd be happy. Ben will be able to walk."

Dylan wiped his face. "That's great, except for one thing. We don't know if Ben is alive or dead."

DADDY! DADDY! Look at me. I'm in a big hotel with Charlene. We saw helicopters and cars and trains. Daddy, why's Charlene holding that gun? Daddy? Daddy!

"Ben?" Dylan mumbled, rubbing his eyes. He'd been asleep.

"Daddy!"

He rubbed his hand down his face, trying to wake up.

Then he heard a familiar giggle and a whisper. "He's asleep. Daddy, wake up!"

Dylan opened his eyes. Was he dreaming?

"Daddy!" Ben ran toward the bed. Alfred was right behind. He caught him and lifted him up onto the bed.

Dylan couldn't stop grinning. Not even when tears slipped over his eyelids and down his cheeks. "Hey, sport," he croaked.

"Daddy! Charlene was real sad when Alfred came. But I was glad. Did you hurt your arm? Is it making you cry?"

"I'm crying because I love you and I'm glad to see you."

"I love you, too, Daddy." Ben laid his head on Dylan's good shoulder. "I got really tired at Charlene's. But I saw helicopters…and planes…and…" He yawned and stopped talking.

Dylan met Natasha's gaze.

She smiled, but her eyes were rimmed with red. "He's here," she whispered.

He smiled. "Thank you, and thanks for getting Werner down here. If the damn doctors will let me, I can scrub in with him when he operates on Ben." He looked at his shoulder. "At least I can scrub one hand."

He looked around. Alfred stood next to Natasha. Storm was standing behind her. Then he looked back at his son and touched his baby-fine hair. "He's asleep."

Alfred moved to take Ben but Dylan shook

his head. "No way, Alfred. You'll have to wait your turn."

Alfred scowled, but his eyes sparkled.

"Oh, Dylan, I'm so glad," Natasha said.

Storm put his hands on her shoulders and whispered something to her. She acknowledged him by angling her head and smiling.

"Dr. Stryker," Storm said, "we're very happy to be able to bring your son back to you, safe and sound."

Dylan nodded, disturbed by the pang of jealousy that had streaked through him when Storm had laid his hands on Natasha. "So it was Charlene, wasn't it?"

Alfred nodded. "I should have known," he said.

Dylan shook his head. "In a way, it should have been obvious, but we didn't figure it out, either, until just—" He raised his eyebrows at Natasha.

"A couple of hours ago. You slept quite a while."

"What's going to happen to her?"

"That's up to the courts," Alfred responded. "On the one hand, she's spilling her guts about Tom and his little group. On the other, she smuggled explosives into your compound and set them so that they could be detonated remotely. She didn't actually set them off, but she was an accessory. And in the helicopter crash, one of the

CSIs found a portable GPS device. She'd obviously planted it to guide the helicopter to the target, which was Ben's play area. It's blind luck no one was killed."

"And Tom's dead," Natasha said. She stepped to one side and Storm dropped his hands from her shoulders with a little smile.

"Do we know who the group was that Tom was involved with?" Dylan asked, doing his best not to glare at Storm.

"Homeland Security will take over that case. They're being picked up now. I'm certain they'll be prosecuted."

Dylan shifted Ben against his side and looked down at him. His little mouth was open and his soft breaths warmed Dylan's bare skin between the strips of adhesive tape that circled his abdomen and ribs.

Then he looked at Natasha. Her eyes were on Ben and the smile on her face was positively angelic. She blinked and a crystal sparkling tear slid down her cheek.

Storm shifted his weight to his other foot. "Well, I'd better get back to the local FBI office. Charlene will be arraigned tomorrow. After that Gambrini and I will head back to D.C."

Natasha turned to him and kissed him on the cheek. "I'll see you back at the office. Tell Agent

Gambrini thank you for me." She pointed her finger at him. "And behave!"

Storm flicked her nose, then shook Dylan's hand and Alfred's. "It was a pleasure to work with you both," he said.

Dylan nodded, and Alfred walked out with the FBI agent.

Dylan looked at Natasha.

"What's the matter?" she asked tentatively. "Everything's all right now, isn't it?"

He shook his head. "Not everything."

Natasha frowned at him. He was still pale, still weak, but the blue fire was back in his eyes. He denied it, but she knew he was upset about something, and that something had a lot to do with her.

"Sit down." It was a command, not a request.

She sat. "Yes, sir."

"Is there something between you and Agent Storm?"

"Something…" She paused, confused, then grinned. "Oh. Well, yeah, if you count a constant battle to keep Storm's mind on the job and off of flirting."

"So you're not—"

Her grin faded and she frowned at him for a second before understanding dawned. "No, we're not. He's a talker and a flirt, but in reality he's like the big brother I never had. Why?"

"Big brother."

Her smile came back. "Yeah. He flirts with everybody. It's his way of keeping his distance— a cover for his inability to commit."

Dylan looked dumbfounded. "What?"

"Never mind." She waved a hand. "What's with all the questions?" She'd like to think he was asking because he wanted her himself, but she knew his entire focus was on Ben right now. And that was the way it should be.

He had his son back. There was no room in his life for anything else. Not now. Maybe never.

As if he knew what she was thinking, he looked down at Ben and shifted his weight a bit.

"Do you want me to take him? You look tired."

"No." He leveled a gaze at her. "I want to ask you something."

"Okay." She steeled herself.

"Are you all right?"

Her heart sank. She'd known that was what he was going to say. She had no idea why she was so disappointed? "Sure. I'm fine. You're the one you should be worried about."

He nodded and looked down at Ben again. "I am. I'm worried about me and Ben and Alfred."

Ben stirred. "Daddy?" He lifted his head. "What's for supper?"

Natasha smiled, blinking back tears. She was

going to miss him—and his father. The hollow empty place in her heart that Dylan and his son had filled began to ache. Soon it would be empty again.

"Tasha!" Ben sat up, digging his elbow into Dylan's side.

He winced. "Whoa, sport. Move slowly. Daddy's got a boo-boo."

Ben giggled. "Grown-ups don't get boo-boos, do they, Tasha?"

She smiled. "Oh, sometimes they do. Sometimes grown-ups' boo-boos aren't on the outside."

Ben cocked his head and frowned, as if trying to understand what she'd said.

"Well, Ben, I've got to go. Your daddy needs rest, and I've got reports to fill out and packing to do." She stopped. "Oh. I guess there's not anything to pack."

Dylan shook his head sadly. "It's all a big pile of rubble now."

"Don't go, Tasha. Stay with us. We can have fun."

She stepped over and held out her arms. Ben sat up and she picked him up. "*Oof,* you are heavy, Ben." She tucked him in the curve of her arm, his lightweight braces resting easily, naturally against her side.

"Charlene fed me a *lot*. But, Tasha, don't go. We want you to stay, don't we, Daddy?"

"That'd be great, but Tasha has a job in Washington, D.C."

Ben looked up at her sadly. "Is Washingdy C a long way?"

"It's pretty far."

"We can go, though. Daddy? Can't we go?"

"Son, there are lots of problems with that. People can't just pick up and move." His gaze met hers and she saw a question there.

"That's right, Ben," she said. "Sometimes, people have to stay where they are. That's where their home is and their life and their work."

"Daddy, me and Alfred'll go, too. We can have a home and a life."

Natasha smiled and kissed Ben's cheek. "You are so sweet. I'd love to take you with me. You could stay with me and we'd have fun. But your daddy needs you here."

"Daddy can go. You like us, don't you?"

She raised her gaze to Dylan's. "Yes, very much."

"Daddy? You like Tasha. You said so."

Dylan rolled his eyes, then smiled. "Yes I do like Tasha."

"Okay." Ben looked pleased with himself.

"From the mouths of babes," he said, smiling tentatively. "Bring him here," Dylan said, holding out his good arm.

Natasha lowered Ben next to his father on the

emergency room bed. He hugged his child to him and ruffled his hair.

"Sit," he said to her, nodding at the side chair.

She sat and clasped her hands in her lap, noticing they were trembling.

"What about it, Tasha? Want to have a home and a life?"

She gaped at him, trying to sort out his words. "A home and a life? What are you talking about?"

"I'm talking about just what you said. A home, a life, work. What do you say?"

"I—I'm not sure what to say."

He raised his brows. "Special Agent Rudolph doesn't know what to say?"

"No. I mean yes. I mean—" She stopped, her cheeks burning. Too afraid to make an assumption in case she was wrong.

Dear God, don't let me be wrong. "I don't think I know what you're saying."

His face turned serious and his expression softened. "I'm asking you to marry me."

She'd have sworn her heart hit the floor. She couldn't breathe, couldn't speak. She sucked in air, forcing her lungs to work. "Have you been hitting the morphine button?"

He chuckled. "No, I haven't been hitting the morphine button. And before you ask, yes, I do know what I'm saying."

She leaned closer. "I don't think it's a good idea for us to get married just to give Ben a mom," she whispered.

"That's not why I'm asking," he whispered back.

"It's not? You mean you—"

"I mean I'm in love with you. I think I have been since the first time I saw you."

Her throat closed up. "I never thought—" she croaked.

"You never thought I'd ask?"

She laughed. "I never thought I'd get married."

"Well?"

"I fell in love with you in the tunnel-house, when you told me what you were afraid of. I just can't believe you love me."

"Believe it. Now kiss me."

She leaned over the bed and kissed him. His good hand cradled her head and his kiss wasn't a sickbed kiss. It was an erotic lovers' kiss.

"Hey," he said against her mouth. "What's this?" He touched her cheek with a finger. "More tears?"

"Happy tears."

"Well, before you get too happy there is one condition."

"Oh?" She couldn't stop smiling, but her heart did a little anxious jump.

"Yeah, if we're moving to D.C. it's going to be your job to tell Alfred. I don't have the courage."

Before he finished the sentence, Alfred came into the room.

"Alfred!" Ben shouted, holding out his arms.

He picked Ben up and bounced him in the air. "What's up, pardner?"

"Tasha and Daddy are going to get a home and a life."

Alfred's eyes snapped from one to the other. "Is that right? Don't I get any say in this?" His face was stern but his eyes sparkled.

Natasha smiled at him. Alfred just wanted Dylan to be happy.

Convincing him to move to D.C. would be a piece of cake. She knew him. As long as he had an escape route, he'd be happy.

* * * * *

Silhouette® Romantic Suspense
keeps getting hotter!
Turn the page for a sneak preview of
Wendy Rosnau's latest **SPY GAMES** *title*
SLEEPING WITH DANGER

Available November 2007

Silhouette® Romantic Suspense—
Sparked by Danger, Fueled by Passion!

Melita had been expecting a chaste quick kiss of the generic variety. But this kiss with Sully was the kind that sparked a dying flame to life. The kind of kiss you can't plan for. The kind of kiss memories are built on.

The memory of her murdered lover, Nemo, came to her then and she made a starved little noise in the back of her throat. She raised her arms and threaded her fingers through Sully's hair, pulled him closer. Felt his body settle, then melt into her.

In that instant her hunger for him grew, and his for her. She pressed herself to him with more urgency, and he responded in kind.

Melita came out of her kiss-induced memory of Nemo with a start. "Wait a minute." She pushed Sully away from her. "You bastard!"

She spit two nasty words at him in Greek, then wiped his kiss from her lips.

"I thought you deserved some solid proof that I'm still in one piece." He started for the door. "The clock's ticking, honey. Come on, let's get out of here."

"That's it? You sucker me into kissing you, and that's all you have to say?"

"I'm sorry. How's that?"

He didn't sound sorry in the least. "You're—"

"Getting out of this godforsaken prison cell. Stop whining and let's go."

"Not if I was being shot at sunrise. Go. You deserve whatever you get if you walk out that door."

He turned back. "Freedom is what I'm going to get."

"A second of freedom before the guards in the hall shoot you." She jammed her hands on her hips. "And to think I was worried about you."

"If you're staying behind, it's no skin off my ass."

"Wait! What about our deal?"

"You just said you're not coming. Make up your mind."

"Have you forgotten we need a boat?"

"How could I? You keep harping on it."

"I'm not going without a boat. And those guards out there aren't going to just let you walk out of here. You need me and we need a plan."

"I already have a plan. I'm getting out of here. That's the plan."

"I should have realized that you never intended to take me with you from the very beginning. You're a liar and a coward."

Of everything she had read, there was nothing in Sully Paxton's file that hinted he was a coward, but it was the one word that seemed to register in that one-track mind of his. The look he nailed her with a second later was pure venom.

He came at her so quickly she didn't have time to get out of his way. "You know I'm not a coward."

"Prove it. Give me until dawn. I need one more night to put everything in place before we leave the island."

"You're asking me to stay in this cell one more night...and trust you?"

"Yes."

He snorted. "Yesterday you knew they were planning to harm me, but instead of doing something about it you went to bed and never gave me a second thought. Suppose tonight you do the same. By tomorrow I might damn well be in my grave."

"Okay, I screwed up. I won't do it again."

Melita sucked in a ragged breath. "I can't leave this minute. Dawn, Sully. Wait until dawn." When he looked as if he was about to say no, she pleaded, "Please wait for me."

"You're asking a lot. The door's open now. I would be a fool to hang around here and trust that you'll be back."

"What you can trust is that I want off this island as badly as you do, and you're my only hope."

"I must be crazy."

"Is that a yes?"

"Dammit!" He turned his back on her. Swore twice more.

"You won't be sorry."

He turned around. "I already am. How about we seal this new deal?"

He was staring at her lips. Suddenly Melita knew what he expected. "We already sealed it."

"One more. You enjoyed it. Admit it."

"I enjoyed it because I was kissing someone else."

He laughed. "That's a good one."

"It's true. It might have been your lips, but it wasn't you I was kissing."

"If that's your excuse for wanting to kiss me, then—"

"I was kissing Nemo."

"What's a nemo?"

Melita gave Sully a look that clearly told him

hat he was trespassing on sacred ground. She was about to enforce it with a warning when a voice in the hall jerked them both to attention.

She bolted away from the wall. "Get back in bed. Hurry. I'll be here before dawn."

She didn't reach the door before he snagged her arm, pulled her up against him and planted a kiss on her lips that took her completely by surprise.

When he released her, he said, "If you're confused about who just kissed you, the name's ully. I'll be here waiting at dawn. Don't be late."

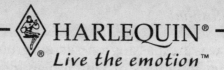

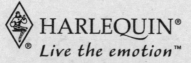

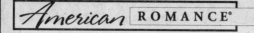
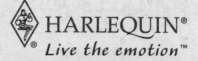

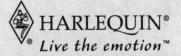

HARLEQUIN® *Presents*

The world's bestselling romance series...
The series that brings you your favorite authors,
month after month:

Helen Bianchin...Emma Darcy
Lynne Graham...Penny Jordan
Miranda Lee...Sandra Marton
Anne Mather...Carole Mortimer
Susan Napier...Michelle Reid

and many more uniquely talented authors!

Wealthy, powerful, gorgeous men...
Women who have feelings just like your own...
The stories you love, set in exotic, glamorous locations...

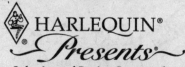

HARLEQUIN® *Presents*

Seduction and Passion Guaranteed!